# THE DETECTIVE

## A NATHAN MCNAMARA STORY

A STANDALONE FROM THE SOUL SUMMONER SERIES

### ELICIA HYDER

Detective Nathan McNamara is one of the leading men in the #1 bestselling series The Soul Summoner.

**The Soul Summoner Series** is available wherever books are sold online: Amazon, Apple iBooks, Barnes & Noble, Kobo, and more!

*"Words cannot describe how enjoyable I found this story. The Soul Summoner is witty, clever and fast paced... Really, this book has it all: Characters you fall in love with, an exciting and unpredictable storyline and humor."* - Juliet Lyons

*"The Soul Summoner is an incredible read. Easy dialogue. Intriguing mystery. A spicy love triangle. It will leave you asking, 'When is the next book in the series coming out?'"* - M. Robinson

*"The Soul Summoner, by Elicia Hyder, caught my interest in the first two chapters and never let go."* - RK. Close

Copyright © 2016 Elicia Hyder

For More Information:
www.eliciahyder.com

For Bridgett...
I'll swim with the bull sharks anytime with you.

# ONE

I'VE NEVER BEEN a one-night-stand kind of guy, but the blonde currently drooling on the pillow beside me might not believe it. *God, what's her name? Lauren? Sharon?*

In truth, if the blistering pain in my skull was any indication of how much Crown I'd put away, I was lucky to be lying next to her and not the geriatric bartender who called me 'Sweet Cheeks' all night. At least the blonde—slobber and all—was hot.

Judging from the foreign, personal furnishings of the room, we'd decided on her place after the bar, rather than my hotel room. There was a lot of pink surrounding me, and stuffed animals. Both good signs that a man didn't live with her. Not that I cared about her relationship status beyond not

having to get in a fist fight before coffee. That
would suck.

My cell phone was laying on the
carpet between my olive drab ball cap and a
flowery high heel shoe. The notification light
was blinking blue, indicating a missed call—or
seven, as I discovered when I picked up the
phone. Gripping the phone with my teeth, I
quietly tugged on my dark green tactical
pants. Sleeping Beauty snorted.

Creeping like a soldier through a
minefield, I tiptoed out of the bedroom and
prayed the chick didn't have a roommate—or
parents—that I would have to deal with. It
was a one-bedroom apartment, thank God.
And aside from us, it was empty. Or so I
thought.

As I slipped silently through the
apartment on a quest for the kitchen, I looked
at my phone. It was almost ten in the
morning. I flipped through the icons on the
screen till I found my voicemail. I clicked play
and pressed the phone to my ear. At the end
of the hall was a living room and a dining
room. *What the hell? Where's the damn kitchen?*

I stopped and leaned against the back
of the tan sofa.

The first message was from my boss. "Nate. I need your report on the Kensington case. Call me."

*Delete.*

"Hey, Noot-Noot, it's Mom. It's about six o'clock on Friday night. Call me when you have a sec, OK? Hope you're having a nice trip to the mountains. Love you. It's Mom. Did I say that? OK, bye."

*Delete.*

I looked around the room. There was no way I was calling my mother till I got back to the hotel.

The next message was from the lieutenant again. "Found the report. Call me back."

*Delete.*

"Hey. It's Mom again. I'm about to go to bed. I guess I'll talk to you tomorrow. I hope everything's OK. Love you, Noot."

I sighed. *Delete.*

"Hey Nate, it's you. The chick's name is Shannon."

I laughed. Out loud. Gotta love drunk me watching out for sober me.

*Delete.*

"Nathan, it is now eight in the

morning, and I still haven't heard from you. I'm starting to worry. Call me."

*Delete.*

Another message. "Oh, I forgot. It's Mom."

I rolled my eyes. "I'm twenty-nine years old," I grumbled.

The final message was from an unknown North Carolina number. "Good morning, Detective McNamara. This is Sheriff Davis calling about the information you were looking for. I've got everything ready for you at my office if you want to come by and pick it up. I'll be here till around eleven."

I looked at the clock again. "Crap."

At the far end of the room was another door that had somehow been camouflaged by my hangover. I rubbed my tired eyes and headed for it. It was a sliding door that easily slipped into the wall, and the light was on in the kitchen. Before my eyes could adjust, an explosion of chaos detonated at my feet.

I stumbled back a few steps as the sound of furious pink toenails, clacking and scraping across the tile floor, ricocheted around the apartment. I covered my ears as a deafening series of yaps ripped through my already-pounding brain. The little yellow dog —Satan in a rhinestone collar—nipped at my ankles as it barked me into the corner.

"Shut up!" I yelled, suppressing the urge to kick the angry ball of fur in self-defense.

The dog bared its teeth at me and growled, daring me to move. When I did, I swear to God, the thing screamed at me before barking again.

Shannon—*Thanks, Drunk Me*—raced into the room, clutching the bed sheet around her. Her hair was wild, like it had been through an AquaNet typhoon, and black mascara was smeared across the side of her pillow-lined face. "Baby Dog!" she scolded, running to save me from the twelve-pound terrorist.

I pointed at the animal. "That dog has rabies!"

She scooped the pooch up into her arms, carefully clinging to the sheet. "She doesn't have rabies." She rubbed her nose against the dog's snout. "You don't have rabies, do you, Baby Dog?" She cooed like it was a baby and not a demon.

*It's a good thing she's hot.*

When she finished making out with her dog, she looked at me. Her eyes dropped to my shirtless torso and grew three sizes. She pinched her lips together, probably to keep her jaw from hitting the floor. *Like what you see, huh?* If I hadn't been so hungover, I would've been tempted to flex.

She pointed her finger at me. "Your fly's open."

I withered.

After adjusting things, I zipped my pants and ducked my shamed head into the kitchen. "Mind if I get some water?"

"There are bottles in the fridge," she said, following me.

Her refrigerator was stocked with drinks, fruit, leftovers, eggs, yogurt…My fridge at home had beer and Gatorade. I retrieved two waters and turned to offer her one. Satan growled at me again.

"So, I had fun last night," she said, hugging the dog closer to her chest.

"So did I." *Apparently.* "Do you have any ibuprofen?"

She smiled and jerked her thumb toward the door. "Yeah. It's in the bathroom.

I'll run get it."

I silently hoped she would glance in the mirror while she was in there.

She barricaded the pup back in the kitchen, and I followed her back down the hall and walked into her bedroom. While I picked up my clothes, a horrified gasp came from the bathroom. I chuckled.

When Shannon finally came back out wearing a pink robe, I was dressed and putting my boots back on. Her hair was tied in a neat ponytail and she was wearing makeup. I could have definitely done worse at the bar.

She swayed her hips sheepishly from side to side. "No time for breakfast?"

I shook my head and stood up. "No. I've got to swing by the sheriff's office before I go check out of my hotel."

She visibly deflated. "That's right. You're leaving today."

I nodded as I adjusted the grayscale American flag patch on the front of my hat. "Yeah."

"What's at the sheriff's office?"

I pulled my hat down low over my eyes and checked to make sure my wallet and badge were still in the back pocket of my pants. "I'm working on a missing person's case in Raleigh, and I think a victim from here might be related to it."

"That's fascinating," she said with a sing-song sigh.

I was pretty sure she would have said the same thing if I'd told her I was here to dig septic lines for the city. I jingled my keychain. "I've got to head out."

She smiled, sort of. "I'll walk you out."

I really wished she wouldn't.

As we passed through the living room, she picked up a business card off the coffee table and handed it to me. It didn't look official. Her name was Shannon Green. "WKNC News?" I turned it over in my hand.

She did a little curtsy thing. "I'm a reporter."

I smiled. "You look like a reporter." I tucked the card into my back pocket. "I'll be in touch," I lied as I opened the front door.

"It was nice to meet you, Detective."

"You too, Shannon."

The mountain air was nearly frozen, and I zipped up my thick coat in the breezeway as she watched from the door. The cold must have finished sobering me up because my brain clicked on. I shook my head and turned back around to face her. "We took a cab here last night, didn't we?"

"Oh!" She laughed. "Yes, we did!"

I sighed. "At least we were responsible."

"I can drive you," she offered.

I checked the time again. The sheriff was leaving his office in twenty minutes. "I've got to be at the sheriff's office by eleven."

She smiled. "Give me five minutes."

*On what planet?* I wondered but kept my mouth shut.

We pulled into the parking lot at the Buncombe County jail with two minutes to spare. I must admit, I was a little impressed. There was an SUV parked in the spot labeled 'Sheriff' and I relaxed. "I'll hurry," I said, wrenching the passenger's side door open.

She turned off the engine. "I'll come with you."

I couldn't object without being a complete jerk, so I didn't and she followed me inside. Behind the welcome desk was a large black woman wearing a blue uniform that was at least two sizes too small. She was smirking before I ever even opened my mouth.

"I'm Detective Nathan McNamara from Wake County, and I'm here to see Sheriff Davis," I said.

"You don't look like no detective." She stood and looked me up and down. "You're too baby-faced and blond to be a detective."

Maybe charm would work. I winked at her. "He's expecting me."

"You got somethin' in your eye, blondie?" she asked, clearly unimpressed by me.

I sighed and pulled out my badge and identification. "Will you please let the sheriff know that I'm here?"

"Sheriff don't take no meetings on Saturday." She leaned forward and sniffed the air. "You been drinkin'?"

I wanted to slam my forehead against the desk. "No ma'am."

She pointed a long red fingernail at Shannon. "She been drinkin'?"

I looked at the woman's name tag. "Ms. Claybrooks, is it?"

She put her hand on her shelf of a hip.

"Please call the sheriff."

Just then, the heavy metal door behind her slid open, and the sheriff stepped into the lobby. "Detective McNamara, glad you could make it!" He held up the white cardboard box in his arms. "I was just about to leave this with Ms. Claybrooks for you."

I was glad he didn't. She'd probably put me through a stress analysis test before giving it to me. I took the box from him and tucked it under my arm. "Thanks, Sheriff."

He nodded. "I hope it's helpful." He crossed his arms over his chest. "Did you have any luck meeting with the Bryson family yesterday?"

My shoulders slumped. "No. I spoke with the mother on the phone, but she wasn't interested in talking to me. I left my number with her in case she changes her mind."

The sheriff shook his head. "It's a terrible thing they went through."

I nodded. "I completely understand." And I did.

He noticed Shannon behind me. "Is that...?"

I took a step to the side. "Sheriff, this is my friend, Shannon Green."

He reached out his hand toward her.

"Yes. The weather girl from channel four."

She shook his hand. "Morning traffic," she corrected him. She straightened her posture and saluted him. "Get the green light with Shannon Green, WKNC Asheville!"

My eyes widened. Sheriff Davis laughed. Shannon started giggling.

"I watch you every morning," the sheriff said. He reached over and squeezed my shoulder. "So, you're close with this fine young man, then?"

She batted her eyelashes up at me. "Quite."

The sheriff looked at me. "Well, maybe you can help me convince him to take a job here in my office."

I heard her suck in a sharp breath. "That would be wonderful."

*Oh boy.*

I laughed to avoid saying anything inappropriate. "That would be something." I looked at my watch. "Well, Sheriff, I've got to check out of my hotel by noon, so I need to get moving." I gestured toward the evidence box. "Thanks again for making me copies of all these reports."

He stuck out his hand. "I hope it helps, Detective. I'm sorry your time here wasn't as productive as you'd hoped." He pumped my fist a few extra times and eyed me carefully. "Think about my offer."

I nodded. "I will, sir."

The sheriff tipped an imaginary hat toward Shannon. "It was lovely to meet you, Ms. Green."

She beamed at him. "You too, Sheriff."

As we walked back out to her tiny sports car, she looped her arm through mine. "So, you might move here?"

I squinted up toward the sun. "Don't count on it, sweetheart."

She leaned into me. "What about just to visit?"

"I don't have much time these days for a social life," I told her, and it was true.

If I was correct about the contents of the box under my arm, I now had eleven dead girls to find.

# TWO

THE WAKE COUNTY Sheriff's Office was bustling like usual when I walked in on Monday morning with my coffee in one hand and a stack of case files in the other.

The morning receptionist, Margaret Barker, was typing at her computer. "Good morning, Detective McNamara."

"Morning, Marge. How's the grandbaby?" I asked as I passed by her desk.

"Spoiled already. Did you have a nice weekend?" she asked.

I still wasn't sure. "It was definitely interesting." I turned and pushed the interior office door open with my back. "Have a good day."

"You too," she said over the white rim of her glasses.

# THE DETECTIVE

On the other side of the door, as I turned around, someone slammed into me. Hot coffee sloshed all over the front of my new tan pullover. "Ah, damn it," I muttered, holding my arms out and looking down at the milky brown puddle around my boots.

"Sorry, Nate!" It was our IT guy, Ramon Edgar. Ramon reminded me of a Weeble Wobble with a soul patch. He had an incurable case of acne that had scarred his face, and he had gauges in his earlobes. He lived in his grandmother's basement and spent his free time playing World of Warcraft. How did I know? Because it was my job to know useless information about people.

I huffed and wiped my shirt with my sleeve. "It's OK, Ramon."

"I got it, boss," someone said to my right. An inmate trustee, Dennis Morgan, was already coming in my direction with a mop.

Ramon was still horrified in front of me. "Man, I'm sorry. I didn't see the door open in front of me."

I held up the files in my hand to silence him. "It was an accident, Ramon. Don't worry about it."

He was fidgeting, paralyzed in limbo

between some unseen further obligation to me and his own social awkwardness. Fidgeting drove me nuts.

I pointed down the hall. "You can go now."

He nodded. "Right. Sorry."

"Need some more coffee?" Dennis was eyeing my empty cup as he sloshed up my spilt drink. His red hair, red eyebrows, and red freckles made his orange and white jumpsuit look like central Florida camouflage.

I stepped over the puddle. "I'm good. Thanks, Dennis."

"Just doing my job," he replied.

"McNamara!" a familiar voice barked across the room. It was the voice that made my balls jump back up into my stomach. Lieutenant William Carr was the resident asshole of the department. He was also my boss.

Carr was standing in the doorway of his office still wearing his long, black overcoat.

I groaned and headed in his direction. "Morning, Lieutenant."

He didn't greet me. "Where are we at with Kensington?" He turned on his heel and walked back into his office while I followed.

He walked around behind his large oak desk and slipped off his coat.

"Sir, we're following up on two leads that we believe are——"

"Do I smell hazelnut?" he asked, adjusting his glasses.

I sighed. "Coffee accident."

His eyes narrowed. "I hate hazelnut."

It was all I could do to not roll my eyes. "My apologies." I approached his desk and offered the files in my hand. "I will personally be following up with Mayor Kensington first thing this——"

He pushed the files away and slammed his fist down on the desk. "While you were off working on your little side investigation, there was another robbery this weekend, Detective!"

My eyes widened. "I'm aware, sir. I got the call this——"

"And what have you done about it? Or do real investigations in this office just not matter to you anymore?" He leaned his arms on his desk and glared at me.

My mouth was hanging open, incapable of forming a response.

A man cleared his throat behind me,

and before I could turn around, Carr's immediate shift in demeanor told me that Sheriff Lyle Tipper had entered the room.

My whole body relaxed.

"Good morning, Bill," the sheriff said. "Detective McNamara."

I turned toward him. "Good morning, Sheriff."

Tipper was the sheriff who hired me fresh out of Basic Law Enforcement Training when I was twenty. He was grayer now and shorter somehow, but he was still a pit bull when he needed to be—and Carr knew it.

"I need to borrow Detective McNamara if you don't mind, Bill." He put a hand on my shoulder.

I enjoyed watching Carr squirm.

He nodded. "Whatever you need, Sheriff."

Sheriff Tipper smiled. "Thank you." He looked at me. "Nate?"

"Absolutely, sir. Lead the way."

The sheriff closed Carr's office door on our way out. "You're welcome," he said before I could thank him.

I wouldn't have thanked him however, because as much as I hated Carr, it would be disrespectful.

"Bill's wound a little tight this morning because the mayor is breathing down all of our throats," he explained.

I wanted to ask him 'what about every other morning?' but I thought better of it. Instead, I just nodded in agreement. "That makes sense. I'm sure the mayor is desperate to know who broke into his home. We are doing everything we can, sir."

Sheriff Tipper smiled. "I know that. How did things go in Asheville this weekend?"

Shannon's bride-of-Frankenstein hair flashed through my mind. "Not as well as I'd hoped. The Brysons weren't interested in speaking with me about their daughter's disappearance, but I went through all the files on the case yesterday, and I'm more confident than ever that it's the same perp."

He nodded. "OK. Well, keep me posted on what you find out." We stopped at my office door and he pointed across the room to where the trustee was still polishing up my mess on the floor. "Who's the new trustee?"

"His name's Dennis Morgan. He's doing eight months for hacking into the county hospital system and erasing the outstanding medical bills for his father and about twenty other terminal cancer patients."

The sheriff pinched his lips together like he was trying to suppress a grin. He just nodded and slapped me on the back. "Have a good day, Detective." His head tilted back in the direction of the lieutenant's office. "And don't mind, Carr. He's all bark." With a wink, he was gone.

Once inside my office, I dropped the files on my desk and flopped down in my chair. It wasn't even eight A.M. yet and it was already a lousy day. I pulled off my olive green ball cap and dropped it on my desk.

"Nate!" The booming voice at my door startled me.

I smiled as Tyrell Reese walked into the room. Reese was my closest friend on the force and my favorite cop to work with in our Investigation Unit. Not just because he towered over everyone, including me, at 6'3 and always had my back but because he was one of the funniest dudes I knew.

"What's up, man?" I asked.

"Nada," Reese said, dropping into the chair opposite my desk. "How was your weekend?"

"Interesting." I laughed and scratched my head.

Reese pointed at me. "You got laid."

I sat back in my chair. "How could you possibly know that?"

He laughed and held up his phone. There was a picture of Shannon and I together at the bar on his screen, and it was sideways and my tongue was hanging out. "I got this at three in the morning." He chuckled. "It wasn't that hard to figure out."

I slid my hand down my face. "Man, I was trashed."

He nodded. "I can tell. What happened?"

I laced my fingers together behind my head and leaned back in my chair. "I went to this sports bar Friday night to watch the game and a couple of the guys from Buncombe County were there. I switched from drinking beer to Crown somewhere during half-time, and it all went downhill from there."

His head snapped back with surprise. "Or uphill. That chick is smoking'."

I smiled. "She wasn't bad."

He slapped his large hand down on

my desk. "I'm proud of you. You needed a night off. All you do is work, work, work."

I pointed at him. "Somebody's gotta make up for your slacker ass."

"Slacker ass?" He leaned toward me. "Who was working B & E's this weekend while you were off banging the beauty queen?"

"I got an earful about it from Carr as soon as I walked in this morning. What have you got?" I asked.

"They hit Cary on Friday," he said. "Over in Preston Bluffs."

I sighed and shook my head. "No shit?"

He nodded. "Took our guys thirty minutes to get there. Mr. Sider was long gone by the time we showed up."

"Sider," I repeated with a chuckle. "Why thirty minutes?"

He turned his palms up. "Closest unit was tied up."

I groaned. "That's starting to become a common theme."

"Yep. Thought so too," he said.

My office phone beeped. "Detective McNamara?" Marge asked over the speaker.

# THE DETECTIVE

"Talk to me," I answered.

"There's a Shannon Green on line three for you."

# THREE

REESE WATCHED MY face melt. "Who?" he asked.

I pointed at the phone and lowered my voice. "The chick from the bar."

He laughed. "Seriously?"

"Put her through, Marge." My phone started ringing, and I looked at Reese. "Can you excuse me for a minute?"

He sat back in the chair and crossed his boot over his knee. "Hell no. I don't wanna miss this."

I wadded up a sheet of paper and threw it at him.

On the fifth ring, I picked up the phone. "Detective McNamara."

"Nathan?" she asked.

"Yes. Can I help you?"

Reese was chuckling across the desk.

"Nathan, it's Shannon." After a pause she added, "Shannon Green."

"Oh, hi." I swirled my index finger next to my ear and mouthed 'this chick is crazy' to Reese. "Is everything OK?"

She sounded bubbly on her end of the line—too bubbly before nine in the morning. "I'm sorry to bother you at work. I just wanted to let you know that you left your watch at my apartment."

I yanked my sleeve back and stared down at my naked wrist. My day just kept getting better and better. "I didn't even realize it." I shifted awkwardly in my seat. "I don't suppose you could FedEx it to me? My mom gave me that watch."

She was silent for a second. "Well, I was thinking I might just bring it to you this weekend."

My mouth dropped open. "Uh…"

"I'm going to be in Raleigh anyway," she added quickly. "I've got an interview with a news station there on Friday morning."

The halogen light above me was flickering like a bad omen. "Uh…sure, yeah. Just let me know when you're in town and we'll hook up."

Reese leaned forward, his eyes doubling in size.

"Why don't you text me your number, so I can get in touch with you on Friday?" she asked.

*This chick is good.*

"OK. Is your cell on the card you gave me?" I asked.

"Sure is!" she bubbled.

"All right. Thanks, Shannon."

"Have a wonderful day, Nathan," she said.

"You too." I quickly slammed the phone onto the receiver before she could say anything else.

Reese was laughing. "Well?"

"She's coming to town this weekend. I left my watch at her apartment."

He smiled at me and cut his eyes in question. "So you could see her again?"

I shook my head. "Definitely not."

"Sure, Nate." He stood up and stretched his long arms over his head. "Whatever you say, brother."

I laughed and pointed to my door. "Get out of my office."

# THE DETECTIVE

When he was gone, I turned on my computer and brought up my case files.

There had been six high profile robberies in our jurisdiction spread out over the first few months of the new year. One or, possibly, two suspects targeted large homes in rural neighborhoods, nothing too far off the beaten path but somehow all conveniently located just out of our immediate reach. The week before, they had hit the home of Albert Kensington—the mayor of Apex. Like the rest of the victims, he and his wife had recently left the home when the thieves broke in. It was unclear whether the mayor was specifically targeted or if it was a coincidence. Thankfully, no one had been injured during any of the robberies, but we all knew that could change at any moment.

The thieves mainly stole cash—all of the victims kept plenty of it in their homes—but at the Kensington residence, they took his whole damn safe. Inside the safe, he kept a notebook full of his passwords to various websites, including his bank account. Before daybreak, $13,000 had been transferred out of his checking and into a web-based account that was opened in the name of Justin Sider, which was funnier and funnier the more I thought about it.

By the time I tracked down Justin Sider's account, it was empty. The money had been withdrawn by Mr. Sider in person from a branch in Virginia. Unfortunately, that bank's cameras were offline that day for maintenance. Whoever the thieves were, they were good.

I picked up the phone and dialed Mayor Kensington's office to tell him I still had nothing to tell him. I prayed it would be enough to keep Lieutenant Carr off my back for the rest of the day.

\* \* \*

After work, I drove out to Durham to visit my parents. Even though it was only thirty miles away from my apartment in Raleigh, it felt like an eternity with rush hour traffic. Raleigh and Durham bled closer and closer to each other as commercial zoning spread out wider each year. It wouldn't be long before there was zero distinction at all. As chaotic as traffic was, it was still the only place I would ever call home. Raleigh-Durham was the only metropolis I knew of where bootlegging moonshine was still considered a profession and whole-hog smoking was a way of life. In fact, I'm pretty sure there was an unwritten rule that in order to be considered a true resident, one had to host at least one annual pig-pickin'. Considering the population, crime was at a minimum, and most acts of violence started and ended with college basketball.

Mom and Dad still lived in the same house I grew up in, on a now coveted thirteen acres just outside the city limits. When I pulled in the gravel driveway of the two-story farmhouse, I parked next to my sister Lara's minivan near the steps of the white front porch.

"Knock, knock," I announced as I walked in the front door.

"In the kitchen!' my mother called out.

I slipped off my boots by the door and walked down the kitchen toward the smell of a roast in the oven. The swinging door from the family room flew open and my three foot nephew, Carter, slid across the hardwood floor in his socks toward me. "Unca Nate!"

I laughed and scooped him up in my arms. "Hey, bud."

He grabbed my nose and pinched it as I carried him into the kitchen. Chocolate—I hoped—was smeared across his cheeks. "Momma says you don't wuv us anymo'ah."

My sister and his mother, Lara, was chopping a tomato on the island. Her mouth fell open. "I said no such thing!"

I blinked with disbelief.

Carter tugged on my nose again. "She says you'ah too busy being a big shot detective to come an' bisit us anymo'ah."

"Is that so?" I asked.

He nodded.

Lara gasped. "Carter!"

I lowered my voice. "Your momma's a little bit coo-koo."

He giggled and covered his mouth with his hands. I kissed his temple before putting him down. He clung to my leg and sat down on my boot.

I looked at my sister. "Talkin' shit, huh?"

"Nathan, watch your mouth!" she shrieked with mock horror.

Mom walked in the back door with a large jar of canned green beans. Her white hair was pulled back and she was wearing the

maroon sweater I'd gotten her for Christmas.
"Hi, son." She came over and kissed my
cheek.

"Hi, Mom."

She pushed the jar against my chest.
"I'm glad you're here. Open this."

I smirked as she walked to the stove.
"It feels so good to be needed."

She laughed. "Oh, shut up. I'm
feeding you, aren't I?"

The jar popped open and let out a soft
hiss. "Yeah, yeah." I handed her the jar.

"Shut up!" Carter repeated.

Lara shook her head. "Nice going,
Nana."

Mom put her hand over her mouth. "I
forgot he was in here."

"Carter, go play in the living room
with your trucks. Nana has a potty mouth,"
Lara said.

Carter obediently got up and ran out
of the room.

Mom looked over at me. "How was
your weekend in Asheville?"

I nodded and leaned against the
counter, producing a pack of Skittles from my
pocket. "It was all right. Not too productive

though," I said as I popped a few candies into my mouth.

"You're going to ruin your dinner, Nathan!" my mother scolded.

I turned the bag up over my mouth and let several pour out onto my tongue. She reached over and smacked me on the stomach. I laughed as I chewed.

"Why wasn't it productive?" she asked. "Was the missing girl's case there not related?"

I twisted the candy closed and tucked it back into my pocket for later. "Oh, I still think it is. It's just the family wasn't interested in talking to me."

She sighed. "Well, I guess I can understand how painful it must be for them."

I kicked my heel back against the cabinet. "I know. You'd just think they'd be excited about someone working on the case again."

She dumped the beans into a pot. "I'm sure they are, sweetheart."

"What's going on?" Lara asked.

I walked over and picked a crouton out of the salad she was making. "I think I've got eleven girls now that were all kidnapped by the same guy."

She put her knife down. "Eleven? Seriously?"

"Yup." I popped the crouton into my mouth.

"That sounds like a job for the FBI," she said.

I nodded. "I'm hoping it will be soon. I'm trying to gather enough evidence that links all the cases together."

She closed her eyes. "Eleven," she said again.

"Where's Dad?" I asked.

Mom put a pan of biscuits in the oven. "He's off with Joe."

I looked at Lara. "With Joe?"

Lara rolled her eyes. "Don't get me started."

"Trouble in paradise?" I flashed her a grin. "Wake Forest?"

She slammed the tomatoes into the bowl hard enough to send some lettuce flying out. "I swear, next basketball season I'm canceling the credit card that those stupid season tickets are connected to."

I laughed and crunched down on another crouton.

College basketball was a big deal in my family—and in most families in the state of North Carolina. My dad, an alumni of NC State, had raised us all as die-hard Wolfpack fans. But within the confines of the Raleigh-Durham lines, two other major schools rivaled us: UNC and Duke. Seventeen percent of all domestic violence crime in Wake County somehow involved the Wolfpack, the Tarheels, or the Blue Devils. And while our family had never been hauled off to the slammer over the NCAA season, basketball was serious family business. Joe—a graduate of Wake Forest, and the only outsider in our clan—was allowed to marry Lara on one condition: that he took Dad to all the Wake/State home games. No joke.

"Hey, Noot, what are you doing on Friday after work?" Mom asked.

Lara rolled her eyes. "Mom, he's thirty. Stop calling him Noot."

Mom walked over and pinched my cheek. "My baby boy will always be my Noot-Noot."

I pointed at my sister. "And I'm not thirty." I quickly did the math in my head. "Not yet, anyway."

"That's right. Your birthday is in a few weeks," Mom said. "What are we going to do for your birthday?"

I winked at Lara. "I was hoping to catch the State game with Joe."

She threw a cucumber at me. "Shut up."

Mom leaned her elbows on the island. "We have to do something special, Nathan."

"Maybe we could take Noot-Noot to the circus and then out for ice cream!" my sister teased.

I laughed. "What's on Friday?" I asked my mom.

She cocked her head to the side. "What?"

My eyebrows rose. "You just asked me what I was doing on Friday."

She laughed and pressed her eyes shut. "Oh yes. Ha, ha." She reached out and gripped my forearm and an earnestness flashed in her eyes that I recognized immediately.

Before she could continue, I shook my head. "No." I knew where the conversation was headed.

She opened her mouth to speak, but I

held up my hand to stop her. "No, Mom," I said again.

She tugged at my sleeve. "Come on. You'll love her!"

"Love who?" Lara asked.

"My friend Valerie's daughter is going to be in town this weekend from D.C. She's a lovely creature, Nathan," she said.

"For the hundredth time, Mom, I don't need you fixing me up with girls."

"Maybe boys, Mom," Lara said with a cheeky grin.

I held up my arms in question. "What are you, twelve?"

Lara laughed and rolled her eyes. "There's no good reason you can't get girls on your own. We just wonder why you never do."

"I had a date this weekend, thank you very much." I regretted the words the instant they left my big mouth.

My mother's eyes were so wide I thought they might pop out of her skull. "Really?"

I nodded. "With a reporter in Asheville." I realized 'reporter' was a stretch.

"How'd you meet her?" Mom pressed.

"We met at a restaurant." OK,

'restaurant' was a stretch as well.

Mom's smile was so bright, I felt instantly guilty. "Well, how'd it go? Are you going to see her again?"

"No, Mom, because she doesn't exist," Lara said.

I glared at my sister. "She's coming to see me this weekend." *What the hell is wrong with me? Shut up, Nate.*

"Ohhhh?" Mom drew the word out into a melodic tune.

I nodded. "But don't get your hopes up. I don't even really know this girl."

"Will we get to meet her?" Mom was clapping her hands together like a sea lion begging for raw fish.

"Mom!"

Lara bumped me with her hip on her way to the refrigerator. "Be careful, Nate. She'll have you married off by dessert."

"You're getting married?" my ten-year-old niece, Rachel, asked. I hadn't even realized she was in the room.

I tossed my hands in the air. "Do you see what you've started, Mom?" I looked at Rachel. "I'm not getting married."

Lara lowered her voice to a snarky

whisper. "Because it's not legal in our state yet."

I grabbed the damp dishtowel and lunged toward my sister. She squealed and ran across the kitchen, grabbing Mom by the arms and using her as a shield. "Mom, make him stop!"

Between Mom's legs, I popped Lara in the shin with the towel. She screamed.

I pointed at her. "Take it back, Lara."

Lara was panting, her blond hair slung across her face. "Put it down, Nathan!"

"Take it back," I said, twisting the towel into a whip again.

"Mom!" Lara screamed and took off running again.

As she rounded the island, I popped her square in the seat of her mom-jeans. She cried out, still laughing, and bolted from the kitchen.

When I turned back toward my mother, she was rolling her eyes. "Sometimes with the two of you, it's like we time-warp back to the 80s." She reached over and yanked the dishtowel out of my hands and started cleaning up the mess Lara had made of the salad.

I laughed. "I know."

"So, tell me about my new daughter-in-law," she said, smiling at me across the island.

I plugged my fingers into my ears. "La! La! La! La! La! La! La! La! I can't hear you!"

She laughed and swatted me with the towel.

# FOUR

FRIDAY MORNING DIDN'T come soon
enough. Not that I was looking forward to
seeing the traffic girl again, but because after a
week of chasing dead leads on the home
invasions, I needed a break—and a beer. I
also really needed my freaking watch back. I
was late for everything all week, including
dinner with Shannon Green at the Bull City
Grill.

I stopped at the hostess station on my
way in.

"How many, sir?" the tiny, not-yet-
legal brunette behind the podium asked.

"I'm looking for someone. Blonde
woman." I wanted to add 'pretentious and
likely overdressed', but I didn't.

The girl nodded. "I think she's at the

bar."

I winked my thanks and crossed the room, weaving my way through the tables toward the bar. I didn't see pretension anywhere. The bartender—forties, fat, caucasian, and balding—leaned his elbows on the bar top. "You look lost."

Shaking my head, I did another scan of the room. "Looking for a girl."

He let out a long, slow whistle, his eyes wide.

I laughed and nodded my head. "Yep, I'm looking for *her*."

He pointed toward a hallway to his right. "Ladies room, I think."

I angled onto a barstool. "Cool. Can I get a beer while I wait?"

"Of course. What'll it be?"

I studied the taps. "Let me try that Goose Island IPA."

"Good choice," he said, retrieving a frosty mug from the freezer.

As he reached to place my beer in front of me, his eyes darted to a flash of red in my peripheral. When I turned my head and saw Shannon Green in a fitted red dress coming in my direction, the world seemed to stop spinning. Everything was in slow motion. Her hair was blown back by an imaginary breeze. The heavens opened up. Angels sang.

The bartender overshot my cardboard coaster, catching just the edge of the mug, and sent it toppling forward on the bar. Swearing as my crotch was doused in frozen IPA, I leapt off my barstool only to plant my feet in the center of the puddle forming on the floor. My right foot slipped, and I crash-landed in a heap by the bar.

Half the restaurant gasped; the other half applauded and laughed. Including my date.

Standing over me, with her hands clamped over her mouth, Shannon's eyes were dancing with amusement. As I hoisted myself up, using the barstool as leverage, she giggled. "I'm sorry. Are you OK?"

I was dripping.

The bartender's mouth was gaping with horror as he thrust a white bar towel in my direction. "Man, I'm so sorry. That was a complete accident."

I nodded and wrung beer out of the front of my fleece pullover. I took the towel and dried my hands. "It's OK."

Shannon offered her hands toward me. "What can I do?"

I jerked my thumb toward the door. "I live about five minutes from here. I'm going to run home and change."

She reached for her black purse that was draped over her shoulder. "I'll come with you."

I opened my mouth to speak, but I closed it and nodded instead. Truthfully, I didn't want to leave her at the bar alone with the reaction she was getting out of every man in the room. Not that I was feeling territorial or anything. I pulled my keys out of my pocket. "You can ride with me."

"OK. Let me settle my tab," she said, turning back toward the bar.

The bartender held up his hand, shaking his head. "It's on me. It's the least I can do for all the trouble I caused."

I wasn't sure how paying for her drinks settled the score between us men, but I nodded my appreciation for the gesture none the less. I looked at Shannon. "Shall we?"

A smile crept across her face, and she looped her arm through mine. Had I not been soaked in booze, my chest would have puffed out with pride as every eye in the room watched us leave.

It was a short drive in a drizzling rain to my apartment, and Shannon's perfume in the close proximity of my truck was making me a little dizzy. "Are you having a good trip?" I asked in an attempt to distract my wandering mind from the way her skirt was scrunched up under her thigh, showing a little more of her leg than she probably intended.

She brushed her hair back off her shoulder. "Yeah. I think my interview went pretty well this morning."

"Oh, yeah. Who was it with?" I asked.

"Wake Up Wake County," she answered.

I nodded. "Good luck with that."

She smiled over at me, and I nearly drove into oncoming traffic.

We reached my apartment somehow in one piece, and she followed me up to the second floor. Once inside, I stripped off my pullover and walked toward the washer and dryer in the hallway. "Make yourself at home. I'll be just a sec."

She looked around my bare apartment. "Uh, OK."

I had a recliner and an entertainment center that took up the whole wall. "I know it isn't much."

"No, it's great," she lied.

I chuckled and started the washer. I dropped the fleece into the machine and stripped off my t-shirt.

"Hey, is that a Glock 38?" she asked.

My mouth fell open as I turned toward her. She was walking over with her eyes on my sidearm. "Yeah. How did you know that?"

She opened her purse and produced a compact 9mm. "I carry the G43."

My heart skipped a beat. "You carry?"

She nodded. "My daddy raised me to not leave home without it."

"Let me see that thing."

Like a pro, she dropped the magazine and cleared the chamber before handing it to me. I might have fallen in love with her right then. "Don't worry, I have a permit," she added quickly.

I chuckled as I handed the gun back to her. "I'm impressed."

She smiled as she reloaded it and tucked it back into her purse. She looked back

ELICIA HYDER

up at me, and I realized I was staring. "Are you going to get dressed?" she asked.

I considered the question for a moment too long, and she pointed down the hallway. "Clothes. Now." She laughed and turned on her heel. "I'm hungry."

I watched her walk to the recliner and sit down, crossing one long leg over the other. *Get a grip, Nate.* "Give me two minutes," I said and walked down the hall.

After changing into a pair of jeans and a black shirt with an army green jacket, I came back to the living room to find that Shannon was gone. "Shannon?"

"In here," she called from the spare room behind me.

I walked back to the second bedroom, which I had converted to a home office, and found her staring at my wall cork board that was plastered with photos of missing women and suspects. I wasn't sure how I felt about her blatant snooping around my house.

As if reading my mind, she said, "I was looking for the bathroom. What is all this?"

I leaned against the door frame. "It's a case I've been working on for a very long time."

She tapped a photo in the center of the board. "I knew Leslie Bryson."

My ears perked up. "What?"

She nodded. "Yeah. We grew up together. Our dads still play golf sometimes. It's a shame they never found out what happened to her."

I blinked. "Seriously?"

She laughed. "Asheville isn't Mayberry, but it certainly isn't a metropolis either." She pointed to all the different photos. "What does she have to do with all these other people? Are they missing too?"

I walked over behind her. "I'm pretty sure that all of these women were abducted and/or killed by the same person. I'm just having a hard time proving it."

She turned to look at me with raised eyebrows. "You think it might be a serial killer?"

"Could be," I answered.

"Yikes," she said. "I remember when Leslie disappeared like it was yesterday. It was so frightening. Stuff like that just doesn't happen in Asheville, ya know?"

"So, you know her family?" I asked.

She nodded. "Yeah. I've known them almost my whole life."

"That's why I was in Asheville, Shannon. I wanted to talk to the family, but they wouldn't see me." I took a step toward her, an interrogation technique to induce stress. "Can you talk to them? Get them to meet with me?"

She sucked in a sharp breath and nodded slightly. "Yeah, I guess so." She reached up and fingered the flap over my jacket pocket. Then she leaned in and cut her sultry eyes up at me. "Does that mean you'll come back to Asheville?"

I gulped. *God, this woman is good.* I took a step back. "Yeah, absolutely."

She giggled. "I'll go see them when I get home tomorrow." She nodded toward the door behind me. "Let's go eat."

We definitely needed to get out of my apartment before I, once again, disproved myself as a gentleman. "Yeah. Let's do that."

"You wanna go back to that bar? Their food looked good," she said as I followed her swaying hips down the hallway.

When we got to my front door, I held it open for her. "No. I wanna take you somewhere nice."

And I did.

Two hours and a hundred dollars worth of steak and wine later, I drove her back to get her car at Bull City. I now knew how she got her job at the news station, why she thinks Legends of the Fall was the greatest movie ever made, and how she tells her daddy she's a Republican but secretly votes Democrat. Aside from the fact that it was the first date I'd had in a really long time, it was surprisingly one of the best ones I'd had *ever*.

As we stood next to her car under the misty glow from the streetlight, her eyes popped open. "Oh! I almost forgot!" She reached into her bag and produced my watch.

I laughed. "I forgot about it too."

Without hesitation, she pulled up my sleeve and draped it over my wrist. As she fastened the clasp she smiled. "I had a really nice time, Nathan."

"I did too. Thanks for keeping my watch safe," I said.

She chuckled, and her phone in her purse began to ring. She pulled it out and looked at it. "Oh my gosh. It's the producer from Wake Up Wake County."

I looked at my watch. It was almost eight at night. "Well, answer it. It's got to be important if they're calling this late."

She was visibly shaking as she put the phone to her ear. "Hello?"

Leaning back against my truck, I watched her face melt from excitement to devastation. My heart began to thump harder in my chest. We'd had a nice date, but I felt an emotionally supportive obligation coming on. And I'm pretty good at a lot of things, but emotional support isn't one of them.

Slowly, she pulled her phone down and pressed the red button to end the call. She stared at it for a moment. "They decided to go with someone else."

*Damn.*

I reached out and pulled her into my arms. "I'm sorry, Shannon."

She laid her head on my chest and sniffed. I was startled by how good it felt when she put her arms around my waist. For a moment, I stroked her golden hair. Pulling back a tad, I looked down at her. "You OK?"

Mascara had streaked her cheeks, and without a thought in my thick skull, I swiped it away with my thumbs. "I'm sorry," she whispered.

My eyebrows scrunched together. "Sorry? For what?"

She gestured to her face. "I'm a mess."

I laughed. "No, the morning we woke up in bed together you were a mess. A few tears is nothing!"

She laughed and buried her face in my chest again. "Oh god," she groaned with embarrassment.

I slid my hands down her arms and took her hands. "I have an idea. Get back in my truck."

She pulled back. Her face was pitiful. "Nathan, you really don't have to try and cheer me up—"

I cut her off. "Shannon, get in the truck."

She smiled and wiped her nose on the back of her hand. "OK."

Twenty minutes later, we were back at my apartment. "Follow me," I instructed, walking down the hallway toward my room.

She hesitated at the front door. "Not to sound rude or anything, but if you're trying to be seductive, it isn't working."

I laughed and turned back around.

"Come on."

Obediently, she followed me to my room. I pulled open a dresser drawer and found a black and red NC State University sweatshirt and a pair of drawstring pants. I held them out for her.

"What is this?" She was eyeing me with clear skepticism.

"You don't have anywhere to be tonight, do you?" I asked.

She shook her head. "Well, no—"

I pushed the sweats against her chest. "Change."

Before leaving my room for her to change clothes, I grabbed my comforter and pillows off my bed. Puzzled, she watched me without saying a word. When I left the room, I closed the door behind me.

In the living room, I moved the recliner out of the way and arranged the bedding on the floor. "I've got to buy a damn couch," I muttered as I walked to the kitchen. I grabbed the carton of ice cream in my freezer and two spoons before walking back to the living room. My feet froze before the rest of my body when I saw Shannon standing in the center of the room wearing my clothes. I nearly toppled over. She giggled and looked down at her outfit. "It's a little big," she said.

"I think it's perfect" slipped out before I could stop myself.

"What are you doing, Nathan?" She looked down at the pallet I'd made on the floor.

I stepped toward the entertainment center and searched my movie shelves. "I couldn't exactly send you off to a hotel all depressed about the job." I peeked back over my shoulder at her. "I don't know you that well. You could jump out the window for all I know."

She laughed and rolled her eyes.

Turning back to my DVD collection, I kept looking till I found what I was searching for. I turned back around with the ice cream in one hand and Legends of the Fall in the other. "Well, I can't make them hire you," I said. "But I do have Brad Pitt and Moose Tracks."

Without a word, she flung her arms around my neck and buried her face in my shoulder. "Thank you, Nathan."

I hooked my arm around her waist and pulled her close. Unable to resist, I kissed the bend of her neck. "You're welcome."

Once again, I woke up with Shannon Green. Only this time, we were on the floor of my living room and both fully dressed. She didn't look like something out of a horror movie and I didn't have a hangover. It was kinda nice. My back, however, reminded me that I was no longer sixteen and that sleeping on floors probably wasn't the best idea. I groaned and arched my back off the floor to stretch the angry muscles.

"Morning," Shannon said, propping her head up in her hand.

"Morning."

"We camped out in your living room."

I laughed. "Yes, we did." I looked over at her. She was pretty cute in the morning when she hadn't passed out drunk the night before. "You feeling better?"

She sighed and smiled. "Yeah. Thanks for cheering me up."

Next to me on the floor, my phone was blinking with messages as usual. There was a text message from Reese on the screen. *Another 10-65 last night. You'd better get your ass to the office.*

I sighed and put the phone back down before rolling toward Shannon. "What time do you have to get on the road?"

She glanced at the clock on the entertainment center. "I've got to check out of my hotel at eleven."

I grinned. "That sounds familiar."

"Yeah, I guess the tables are turned this weekend." She pointed at me. "Including my car was left at a bar last night. I'm going to need a ride."

Dramatically, I rolled my eyes. "God, you're needy!"

"Hey!" She poked me in the stomach, and I grabbed her by the finger.

And that was all it took.

Somehow I'd managed to keep my damn hands to myself and be an upstanding guy all night long, but one poke to the bellybutton was like pressing the NOS injector on a hotrod.

I guess Shannon Green wasn't a one-night stand after all.

# FIVE

LATER—MUCH LATER—at her car, I kissed Shannon goodbye with a promise I'd call. I was almost certain I'd keep it too, then I headed to the office. Lieutenant Carr's truck was in its spot next to the sheriff's. I almost turned around and drove back home.

Marge was at the front desk. "Morning Detective," she said, lowering her reading glasses to look at me.

"It's Saturday, Marge. Shouldn't you be off today?"

She slid a long silver letter opener into the flap of an envelope and sliced it open. "Well, I should be, but I'm not. Are you here because of the robbery?"

I rolled my eyes as I passed by her desk. "I'm here to keep the lieutenant off my ass."

She smirked. "Good luck with that."

The office was hopping when I walked through the door. I tried to slip across the room unnoticed, but Reese spotted me from the coffee pot. "McNamara!" he boomed.

I closed my eyes and silently cursed.

He walked toward me, coffee in hand, chuckling to himself.

At the same time, Carr's head popped out of the doorway to his office. "Detective, I'd like to see you," he called to me.

I knocked Reese in the arm with my shoulder as I passed him. "I hate you, dude."

"He can smell fear, Nate," he warned.

Over my shoulder, I shot him the bird.

Taking a deep breath, I stepped into Carr's office. "Morning, Lieutenant."

Carr was walking back around behind his desk. "Nice of you to join us today, Nathan."

"I've worked almost seventy hours this week, sir," I said.

He cut his eyes up at me. "Is that an excuse?"

I shook my head. "No, sir. Just a fact."

"Do you know how many hours I've

worked this week, Detective?" He folded his hands on top of his desk.

"Nope."

"More than you."

I cringed with mock sympathy. "Then I feel sorry for your wife."

His eyes narrowed. "Get out of my office."

"Yes, sir," I said, not waiting for him to change his mind.

Reese was chuckling outside my office door when I walked back out. "Are you trying to get me fired?" I pulled out my key ring.

"If you do get fired, that look on your face earlier was so worth it," he said. "Where've you been all morning?"

"Home." I unlocked my office door and flipped on the light as Reese followed me in carrying a brown file folder. "I don't understand why it's implied that I'm not doing my job if I'm not here twenty-four hours a day."

Reese sat down in the chair. "You know it's just politics. Lots of money and press putting pressure on this case."

"So, what's the story on this one?" I turned on my laptop.

He crossed his boot over his knee and used his leg as a desk. He rifled through the papers in the folder. "Our latest victims are Max and Juliette Carrera. They own the Chevy dealership out off of Riker Boulevard. Thanks to the little bit of rain yesterday evening, our guys confirmed two sets of muddy footprints in the foyer of the home. Size ten and size ten and a half. The thieves stole $7,000 from a wall safe inside the home office." Reese leaned forward. "They also took an antique 1853 engraved Remington revolver valued at ten G's."

I sat back in my seat. "Really? That's new."

He nodded. "The owner said it was stored in the safe with the money. I think Max was more upset about the gun than anything."

I blew out a sigh. "I would be too." I looked up at the clock on the wall. "Wanna take a ride out there?"

Reese closed the folder and nodded. "Sure."

Standing up, I put my keys in my pocket. "You can drive."

I rode shotgun in Reese's unmarked sedan across town to the Carreras' home and went through our database files on his mounted laptop to see—again—if I'd missed anything. While I searched, I filled him in on the details of my evening with Shannon and the ensuing morning after.

He grinned over his shoulder as he pulled into the golf course community. "So what I hear you telling me, is that you have a girlfriend."

My eyes rolled involuntarily. "I don't have a girlfriend."

He cringed. "You cuddled, man. All night. You definitely have a girlfriend."

"Whatever."

He raised his eyebrows. "You gonna see her again?"

I looked out the windshield. "I'm probably going back to Asheville to meet with the Bryson family this weekend."

He laughed. "Isn't that convenient?"

"Shut up."

We pulled into the driveway of a three-story plantation-style home with a garage that was bigger than the house I grew up in.

Reese let out a long, slow whistle. "I went into the wrong profession," he said, shaking his head.

I wrenched my door open. "You and me both, brother."

When we reached the elaborate front door, I noticed a sticker in the corner of one of the decorative window panes around the entry. I tapped it with my finger. "Daycon Securities," I said. "Is there anything about it in the report?"

Reese rang the doorbell. "Nothing other than it wasn't on at the time."

"That's happened before." I scanned the entryway for cameras. There were none. "Didn't the mayor use Daycon?"

Reese pressed his eyes closed. "Maybe so. You think it might be related?"

I inspected the broken frame around the door, where someone had used a crowbar. "I think it's odd that none of these million dollar homes have had functioning security equipment."

Reese nodded. "True."

The front door opened and a tall redhead in her mid-forties with a boob job and Botox looked out. She had been featured in many of their car dealership's commercials. "Can I help you?" she asked with an arched eyebrow.

Reese flashed the badge that was attached to his belt. "I'm Detective Tyrell Reese from Wake County Sheriff's Office. Are you Mrs. Carrera?"

She smiled politely. "I am." She swung the door wide. "Come in."

As we stepped through the doorway, Reese nodded in my direction. "This is Detective McNamara. He's the lead investigator on this case."

I offered her my hand. "I'm sorry that it's under these circumstances, but it's nice to meet you."

"You too, Detective." She closed the door behind us. "Come on in. Max is actually on the phone with the insurance company right now."

The foyer opened up into an elaborate formal living area with a grand piano, white furniture, and some kind of white fur rug, which I avoided with my boots like my life depended on it because I feared it might. We followed her toward the sound of an angry male voice on the other side of the house. Beyond the white room was a short hallway that came to a dead end in the home office.

The office doors were made of paned glass squares; one of them was shattered.

Inside the room, Max Carrera—5'9, hair plugs, Italian—paced with a cell phone in his white-knuckled fist. His face was red as he barked something about a deductible. After a moment, he registered our presence and stopped wearing a hole in the carpet. "I'll call you back," he said and disconnected the line. He dropped the phone onto the mahogany desk and planted his hands on his hips. "Did you catch them yet?"

I shook my head. "We're still working on it, I'm afraid. Mr. Carrera—"

He cut me off. "Call me Max."

"Max, I noticed you have a pretty hefty security system. Was it not on at the time of the robbery?" I asked.

He huffed. "Teenagers."

His posture indicated that I should know what he meant, but I didn't. "I'm afraid I'm going to need a little more of an explanation."

He pointed a finger toward the ceiling. "We have a sixteen year-old son who is currently grounded for leaving the house last night without turning the system on. He does it all the time."

I sucked in a sharp breath through my clenched teeth. "That's a shame."

Max's frown deepened. "Don't have kids, Detective."

"Max!" his wife shrieked.

I had to suppress a smile. "Tell me about the gun that's missing."

Max exhaled through his nose so hard I heard his sinuses whistle across the room. "It was a gift from my grandfather who bought it off of a gangster in old New York about eighty years ago. It's about a hundred and fifty years old or more." He walked over and handed me a picture of a revolver with a white handle and swirly designs along the silver barrel.

Reese looked over my shoulder. "I can see why you're upset," he said.

Max looked at both of us. "I don't care about the money, but I want my gun back."

I held up the photograph. "Can I keep this?"

He nodded. "Be my guest."

"It was in your safe with the cash?" I asked.

He stepped away from his desk toward the large built-in mahogany bookcase that lined the wall. A panel had been removed from the back casing, displaying an open and empty safe. It was covered in the remnants of fingerprinting dust. "Reese, did we get any prints off this?" I asked.

He consulted the file. "None that didn't belong to Mr. Carrera."

Max held up his hands in defense. "I didn't rob my own house."

I smiled and examined the safe door. "No one is saying you did." I looked back over my shoulder. "There are no signs of forced entry, but these aren't super complicated to crack if you have the right stuff."

Max's eyes doubled in size. "Are you kidding me? Do you know how much I paid for that thing?"

I looked at the safe again. "I would guess around three to four thousand."

Max looked like he might throw up.

I shrugged. "You did better than most I've seen. One guy had a fingerprint reader on his safe that could be disabled if you pressed down too hard when you put your finger on it."

"Well, what kind of safe do you recommend?" He looked ready to take notes.

I slapped him on the back. "I recommend guard dogs and banks." Then I smiled. "And sometimes not even banks."

He offered me his hand and I shook it. "Thanks for coming by, Detective."

I smiled gently. "I promise we're doing everything possible, Max."

He sighed. "At the end of the day it's just stuff, I guess."

I nodded. "I agree, but we're still going to try to get your stuff back."

He squeezed my hand one more time before releasing it. "I'm sure you are."

The Carreras saw us to the door. Once we were outside, I glanced at the security emblem again. When we got in the car, I turned his laptop back around toward me.

"What do you think?" Reese asked.

"I think I want to know more about the security systems. Seems odd to me that none of these million dollar homes have had their alarms set at the time of the break-in. And I want this picture posted at every pawn shop within fifty miles. This gun is going to be easy to recognize."

# THE DETECTIVE

He nodded as he backed out of the driveway.

My cell phone buzzed in my pocket. I yanked it out and read the text message on the screen. *Half-way home. Stopped for lunch. Had a great morning. Can't wait to see you again! <3, Shannon.*

A groan escaped my throat. "Oh boy."

# SIX

THE MORE I looked at the files on the break-ins, the more convinced I was that we were dealing with some serious professionals. Out of the seven homes that had been hit, four safes had been opened without any damage, two had been bounced and their hinges warped, and I suspected they took the Kensington's because they couldn't get it open fast enough. It was one of the more complex safes on the market, so that made sense.

All of the homes had one key component in common: ArmorTech security systems. ArmorTech was the parent company of Daycon Securities, ATR Securities, and HomeSafe Technologies—all of which were used by the victims. I had contacted ArmorTech on Monday morning when I first discovered the connection, but by Thursday they still hadn't found any data leakage on their end.

Thursday night, with my feet propped up on my home office desk and a takeout container of General Tso's chicken balanced on my lap, I stared back and forth between the two bulletin boards on the wall. The one on the left was all the robbery info I had. The one on the right had the faces of eleven missing women tacked to a map of North Carolina.

Neither case was going anywhere.

My phone rang. It was Shannon.

I answered it on speakerphone. "Hello?"

"Hi, Nathan. It's Shannon."

"Hi, Shannon." I popped another bite of chicken into my mouth. She had called twice that week and had texted me steadily since she left town. I still wasn't sure how I felt about it—definitely not sure enough to postpone my dinner for the duration of our conversation.

"How was your day?" she asked.

I swallowed. "Not too bad. Still working. What's up?"

"I wanted to let you know that I spoke to Caroline Bryson today. Leslie's mom."

My boots landed on the floor with a thud as I sat up straight in my office chair. "Oh, really?"

"Yes. She said she would be happy to speak with you, since you're a friend of mine," she said. "She wants to know if you can come back to Asheville this weekend."

*Sure she does.* I could talk to Caroline Bryson on the phone and we both knew it.

I thought for a second. "Yeah, I could drive back tomorrow after work."

I swear to God, I could hear her smiling.

"Great! I'll let her know to maybe plan for Saturday," she said.

"Awesome. Thanks, Shannon."

"Hey, Nathan?"

"Yeah?"

"Do you…um…Do you want to stay with me?" Her voice cracked on the other end of the line.

If I were a better detective, I wouldn't have been surprised by the question. I thought for a second. *Free place to stay, probability of sex…* "Sure, I guess." Then I remembered her damn dog and almost winced audibly.

"Great! I'll text you my address in case you don't remember how to get here," she said, her voice bubbling over with excitement on her end of the line.

"Fantastic. I'll head that way tomorrow after work," I said. "Thanks, Shannon."

"My pleasure. Bye, Nate."

I hung up the phone and stared at it for a long minute.

Reese was right. *I have a girlfriend.*

\* \* \*

It was dark and the sky was spitting snow by the time I pulled up in front of Shannon's apartment building Friday night. My door creaked as I slammed it shut and slung my backpack over my shoulder. On the walk up to her door, I continued my internal deliberation over how I wanted this weekend to play out. 'The Talk' was coming. I could feel it in my bones.

My three sharp knocks on the door triggered the nerve-shattering yelps of Baby Dog who was no doubt lying in wait for me inside the apartment. Even through the thick metal door, I could hear her growling.

The door opened a half a foot, and Shannon was using her leg to barricade the dog inside. Satan was losing her shit, head-butting the back of Shannon's calf as she tried to charge me.

"Your dog hates me!" I shouted over the incessant barking.

She reached down and picked her up. "I'm so sorry." She backed away from the door so I could walk inside.

Baby Dog bared her teeth viciously.

Shannon tried to soothe her ruffled fur. "I'm not sure what's gotten into her!"

I laughed and shook my head, dropping my bag at the door. Shannon carried the dog down the hall and locked her in the bedroom. She was still barking.

I ran my fingers through my frost-covered hair. "Is she like this with everyone or am I special?"

Shannon sighed. "She hates men."

I rolled my eyes. *Great. A cock-blocking canine.*

My nose detected the scent of roasting meat.

"It smells amazing in here. Did you cook?" I asked, unzipping my jacket.

Shannon reached to help me. "Here, let me take your coat."

Surprised, I let her pull my jacket off my arms.

Her blond head tilted in the direction of the kitchen. "I figured you didn't take time to stop and eat, so I made dinner. I hope you like beef stroganoff."

"I like beef anything." I straightened my shirt as she hung my coat by the door. "Thank you."

It was then that I noticed the effort Shannon had put into my visit. The table was set with more plates than we needed. There were candles and a bottle of wine in the center. The apartment looked like it had been professionally cleaned. And Shannon, well... even though she was just wearing jeans and a sweater, Shannon looked like she had just walked off the cover of a magazine. *There could be worse things than having a girlfriend, I suppose.* I stretched my hand toward her, and she blushed as she took it. I pulled her close and kissed her.

She smiled and put her hands on my chest when I pulled away. "Are you hungry?"

"Starved."

The next morning, I awoke to a blond head on my shoulder and snow on the ground outside. It felt good. Damn good—the blonde, not the snow, that is. The snow was cold, very cold, but it wasn't quite deep enough to prevent a trip out to the Bryson's house. Shannon was in the passenger's seat, a spot I was getting used to seeing her in.

When I pulled into the driveway, I surveyed the modest two-story home. "Is there anything I should know?"

She thought for a second. "They still get pretty emotional sometimes talking about Leslie is all, but they are nice people."

I nodded and reached in the back seat for the files I had brought.

Shannon led the walk to the door, and I stood back while she pressed the door bell with her mittens. She looked cute in mittens and earmuffs. I smiled and winked at her.

The door opened and a woman— fifties, plump, and gray—ushered us in out of the cold. "My stars!" she exclaimed, grabbing Shannon by the jacket and tugging her inside. "I expected you two to cancel on account of the weather!"

Shannon slipped off her boots in the

foyer, and I did the same.

"Nathan has four-wheel drive." Shannon gestured toward me. "Caroline, this is Detective Nathan McNamara."

I stuck out my hand, and she shook it. "It's nice to meet you, Mrs. Bryson."

"Please, call me Caroline," she said. "I'm sorry I didn't speak with you the last time you were in town."

I shook my head. "Don't worry about it."

She cleared her throat. "It's just that a lot of people have talked to us about Leslie over the years, and it's always the same thing: we get our hopes up and get disappointed."

"Ma'am, I completely understand." And I did.

Shannon hung up her coat on a rack near our shoes and then took mine.

"Shannon said you were a friend of hers, so I changed my mind." She turned toward the living room behind us. "Come on in. Y'all want some coffee or some iced tea?"

I shook my head. "I'm good, thanks."

Shannon sat next to me on the floral print sofa in the living room. Caroline sank into a rocking chair across from us. "How can

I help you, Detective?"

I leaned forward and rested my elbows on my knees. "I've been investigating two disappearances out of Raleigh that happened about twelve years ago."

She blinked with surprise. "Pardon my bluntness, but you don't look old enough, Mr. McNamara."

I smiled. "I'm not. I've only officially been on this case for around eight years."

She blinked again. "I'm afraid they don't give cases that old much attention around here."

I shook my head. "Most of my work is done on my own time."

Her eyes narrowed in question.

"One of the victims was my younger sister, Ashley McNamara." I opened the file folder and pulled out a picture of my sister. "She was kidnapped after a football game my senior year of high school."

Caroline took the photograph, her mouth gaping and tears forming in the corners of her eyes. "I'm so sorry, Detective."

"Call me Nathan." Out of the corner of my eye, I could see Shannon's wide eyes. I sat back and draped my arm across the back of the couch behind her. "Caroline, I believe that your daughter and my sister may have been abducted by the same person. In fact, I believe Leslie's disappearance is linked with ten other cases."

She covered her mouth with her hand. "Ten others?"

I nodded. "Counting Leslie, there have been eleven girls between here and Raleigh who have all disappeared under similar circumstances. They're all around the same age, and they were taken from public places with no signs of foul play."

She handed the picture back to me. "What does this mean?"

I tucked the picture back into the folder. "I believe that I have enough evidence now to put pressure on the FBI to begin investigating these as a serial case."

Caroline sat forward. "Like a serial killer?"

I sighed and turned my palms up. "It could be a possibility."

Caroline withered in her seat. My heart truly hurt for her.

"Mrs. Bryson, I'm not going to try and fill you with false hope that I can bring your daughter back." I leaned forward again. "But I am asking you, as my sister's brother, to help me not let these cases be cold anymore."

Her face softened. She sniffed and dabbed at her eyes with the sleeve of her shirt. "What can I do to help you, Nathan?"

"Be vocal," I said. "That's really it. Families still have the most influence with local, state, and federal agencies, and the more families we have insisting that these cases be looked into, the better chance we have of someone in authority taking action."

She took a deep breath. "OK."

I smiled. "Thank you." I pulled a business card out of the folder and handed it to her. "This has my cell phone number on it. Feel free to call me anytime."

She accepted the card and smiled. "Thank you for everything you're doing."

"I made a promise to my mother, ma'am. And I don't break promises to my mom," I said.

Caroline pointed at me and smiled at Shannon. "I like this boy. Have your parents met him?"

My blood pressure kicked up about forty points. I could feel my jugular beating against the collar of my shirt.

Shannon giggled and rubbed my back. "No, but I know they would love him."

Caroline stood up. "Well, he has my endorsement, for sure." She pointed toward the kitchen. "Would either of you like some lunch?"

I shook my head as I stood. "No, thank you. I've really got to get back to Raleigh."

Shannon whined and gripped my arm. "No, you can't!"

I laughed. "No?"

She poked out her pink bottom lip. "No." She reached for my hand. "You can stay one more day."

I was sure Lieutenant Carr would argue otherwise.

After a moment, I nodded. "OK. I'll stay." I smiled at Caroline. "Lunch would be great."

# SEVEN

ONCE MY MOTHER learned that I had spent another weekend in Asheville, I was summoned to dinner on Monday night for a full report. On my way out of the office, I passed Reese in the lobby. Skidding to a stop, I looked down at my watch. "You're late for work, bro."

He laughed. "Just getting back from securing warrants for the homicide in Wendell."

"It's going down tonight?" I asked.

He nodded. "Yeah. You coming?"

"Do you need me to?"

He shook his head. "Nah. You just usually like in on these things."

I sighed and jerked my thumb toward

the door. "I'm headed to Mom's for interrogation about my weekend."

He grinned. "How is the girlfriend?"

"Smoking hot."

"Oh yeah?" He crossed his arms over his chest. "No more arguing with me, huh? It's official?"

I shrugged as I zipped up my coat. "Surprisingly, we didn't talk about it. I think she's coming back up this weekend though."

He pointed at me. "I want to meet her this time."

Shaking my head, I pulled my keys out of my pocket. "I don't think so."

"C'mon, man. I promise I won't try and charm the pants off her or anything."

I laughed and rolled my eyes. "Sure you won't."

He looked down at his watch. "I've gotta get going."

"Stay safe tonight," I said as he walked past me.

"Always." He turned back before crossing through the back office door. "Say 'hi' to your mom for me."

"Will do."

When I arrived in Durham, I was

greeted at the door by my mother who was wearing a smile that was almost wider than her face. "Hi, Noot."

I kissed her on the cheek. "Hi, Mom."

"You're late."

I glanced at my watch. "Three minutes."

She took my coat when I slipped it off and hung it by the door before looping her arm through mine and tugging me toward the kitchen. "So, tell me all about her!"

I laughed. "Can I not even sit down first?"

"You'll have time to sit when I'm dead." She pulled on my arm. "How did it go?"

My dad, who looked like me in twenty-five years, was sitting at the breakfast table in the kitchen when we walked in. "Hey, Dad." I walked over and shook his hand. "Long time, no see."

He nodded and put down the newspaper he was reading. "It has been a while, son."

I sat down across from him and took off my hat. "I know. How was the game last week?"

Mom was practically dancing with anticipation beside me.

Dad leaned his elbow on the table. "It was a good game. The team is looking really good—"

Mom squealed, cutting him off. "You can talk about sports later!"

Dad chuckled. "Nate, I think you'd better tell your mother about the weekend before she has a stroke on us."

Using the toe of my boot, I pushed a chair out for my mother. "Sit, Mom. You're making me nervous."

She plopped into a seat with wide-eyes and a perma-grin. "Is she just wonderful? Do you love her?"

Laughing with disbelief, I tossed my hands in the air. "No, I don't love her! I hardly know her." I laughed. "Help me out here, Dad."

Dad shook his head and sipped his glass of iced tea. "No can do. She's been planning the wedding since Friday."

I groaned. "There's no wedding."

Mom pinched my arm. "Not yet."

I rolled my eyes.

"I Googled her on the computer this

afternoon," Mom said. "She's stunning."

With that I couldn't argue. "She is really pretty."

Mom covered her mouth with her hands. "Don't be mad at me."

*Uh-oh.*

"Why?" I sat forward on my seat, recognizing my mother's guilty tone. "What did you do?"

She sucked in a breath through her teeth. "I emailed her at the news station."

My mouth fell open. "You what?"

She turned her palms over. "I couldn't help myself."

I looked to Dad for help. His lips were pinched together in an effort to not burst out laughing. Finally, he shook his head. "I couldn't stop her."

"When?" I grabbed Mom's arm. "What did you say?" My mind was racing. I covered my face with my hands. "Oh god, Mom. What did you say to her?"

She shook her head and flattened her hands on the table. "Nothing bad, sweetheart."

I dropped my face back toward the ceiling. "Of course not."

"I just invited her to come to dinner soon," she said.

I let out a heavy sigh. "Of course you did."

She gently shoved me in the shoulder. "Well, if I didn't, you never would! You never bring your girlfriends over to visit us!"

I held up my hands. "And this is why! I hardly even know this woman, Mom. I'm not ready for her to meet my parents."

She sat back and folded her arms indignantly. "Well, you'd better get over it because she's coming to dinner on Saturday."

I dropped my forehead onto the table. "You've got to be shitting me."

She smacked the back of my head. "Language, Nathan!"

My phone was buzzing in my pocket. I angled sideways and wrenched it out. "That's probably her now, calling to discuss baby names and china patterns."

Dad's shoulders shook with silent laughter.

It was the station.

I pressed the phone to my ear. "McNamara."

"Nathan, you've got a 10-65 in

progress that sounds like your guys," Bernie Davis said quickly on the other end.

I stood up so fast, my chair toppled backwards. "Where?"

"Near Allen Creek Country Club."

"On my way." I disconnected the line. "Sorry, Mom. Gotta go."

She pouted. "But I made your favorite pork chops."

I kissed the top of her head. "Sorry. It's that robbery case I'm working. I'll call you later."

She huffed. "OK. Fine."

I pointed at her as I crossed the kitchen. "But this isn't over. No more contacting Shannon or anyone else I might be dating."

She followed me out of the kitchen. "Nathan Gabriel McNamara, you'd better not be dating anybody else! We raised you better than that!"

"Stay off Google, Mother!" I called to her from the front door as I grabbed my coat.

"Be careful, Nathan!" she replied as I slammed the door behind me.

Inside my truck, my police scanner was a flurry of activity. The scene of the robbery escalated with impressive speed and before I even got to the highway, someone had called in possible gunshots and a fire. The country club was normally only ten minutes away, but it was rush hour and I'd driven my personal truck instead of my unmarked SUV with lights and a siren. I cursed every red light I hit.

When I pulled up in front of the three-story stone house, the second floor windows were leaking black smoke and bright orange flames licked at the glass. The sun was setting and the smoke rising against the horizon created a ghostly fog in the fading sunlight. The fire department beat me there by five minutes.

A crowd had gathered on the front lawn and two other deputies, who had arrived just before I did, were trying to keep them out of the way of the firefighters as they toted hoses and gear at a sprint, to and from the house.

"Where are the homeowners?" I asked one of the deputies, whose name I couldn't remember.

"We just got here, Detective," he answered, holding a couple of teenage boys at bay with his arms.

I put my hands on my hips. "Who called it in?"

"I did!" An older woman—caucasian, early seventies, white hair—was standing beside him. "I live just over there." She pointed to the house to our left. "I called 9-1-1 when I heard some glass breaking, and I saw two men with masks on their heads go in the side door over there. While I was on the phone, there were gunshots inside the house!"

I took a few steps toward her. "Ma'am, who owns this home?"

She looked around the yard. "Dr. Withers. He's a cardiologist over at Duke." She strained her eyes. "But I haven't seen him."

I nodded toward the house. "Do you know if anyone was at home?"

She shook her head. "I don't know. The doctor and his wife split up a few months ago, but his kids still live here. They're in school."

I pulled a pen and a mini notebook out of my jacket pocket. "How old are the kids? Do you know?"

"High school age," she answered.

"Anthony and Carissa, a boy and a girl."

"The men entering the house, can you tell me anything about them?" I held my pen angled, ready to take notes.

"One of them was tall and thin, the other was short and a little plump. They were white, but I could only tell by their hands. They were wearing dark ski masks."

"Did you see how they got here?" I looked around. "Was there a car, or were they on foot?"

She shrugged her tiny shoulders. "I'm not sure. I didn't see a car, but there was a lot going on."

A blue sports car rolled to a stop in the middle of the street and a teenage boy— black, short hair, six feet—stepped out of the driver's side. The fear in his eyes told me exactly who he was. "Anthony Withers?" I took a step toward him.

His gaping mouth didn't respond, but he nodded slightly.

"Anthony, look at me," I said.

He blinked and we made eye contact. "Th-th-that's my house."

I gripped him by the arms to hold his attention on me. "Anthony, do you know if anyone was at home?"

"Uh…" He looked around. "My sister, Carissa, was supposed to come home after school." His eyes were becoming frantic as he searched the crowd. "Where is she?"

I got in his face again. "Anthony, I need you to stay here. I'm going to go and find her." I grabbed the other deputy by the jacket and looked at him seriously. "Keep an eye on him," I said, shoving him toward the frightened kid.

I took off in a jog across the lawn toward the burning home. Two firefighters were carrying the hose toward the front door. "Hey, there might be a girl in the house. A teenager!" I shouted over the commotion.

"They're clearing the house now!" one of them replied, not pausing to look at me.

Another firefighter was up on a ladder to the second floor, using an axe to bust out another window. I was watching him rip the glass out of the frame when someone shouted my name from the front door. A large firefighter dressed in full gear was waving his arms. I ducked through the people coming and going from the front entrance.

"Nathan, it's Rob Burgess!" the man

shouted, lowering his mask so I could see his face. Rob was a captain at the fire department. It wasn't the first time we'd been at the same crime scene.

I shook his hand. "How's it going in there, Rob?"

"I'm afraid we have a fatality."

A boulder, the size of Saturn, dropped into my stomach.

"Looks like the fire was started to cover up a homicide," he continued. "She's burned pretty bad, but she's got an obvious gunshot wound to the head."

I thought I might vomit.

"How soon can I get in there?" I asked.

He nodded back inside. "The fire is pretty well contained to the second floor and we've almost got it under control. I'll keep you posted."

He disappeared back into the house, and I turned back toward the lawn with my radio out ready to call in a homicide. Across the yard, the deputy was still having to restrain Anthony Withers.

His sister was dead and scorched inside the house behind me.

I thought of my little sister, Ashley. Then I turned and puked on the rose bushes.

# EIGHT

CARISSA ANGELIQUE WITHERS had been shot in the head at point blank range in the doorway of her bedroom. She was fifteen. Laying next to her charred frame was a ten thousand dollar murder weapon: a hand-engraved, 1853 Remington revolver.

I'd lost four pounds by Thursday because I couldn't eat. Or sleep.

A few things became clear to me after we'd collected all the evidence from the house fire. These weren't seasoned criminals as I had originally thought. No criminal would carry an antique handgun that hadn't been fired in a century to a robbery. They were lucky it hadn't blown up in their hand. My theory was the gun was taken as a nifty trinket from the safe in the Carreras' home, and it was carried by an amateur, albeit brilliant, thief to the next target. They hadn't expected Carissa to be at home during the time of the robbery, and she was shot by a remorseful shooter because she surprised them. The handgun—complete with a set of at least partial fingerprints—had been discarded and set on fire to cover up the accident because they didn't know what else to do.

The forensics team at the State Crime Lab was working on the gun.

A couple other points were very interesting as well. The home was protected by ArmorTech, and Dr. Withers kept cash in a combination safe inside his home office. The thieves hadn't gotten to it, however. They bolted empty-handed as soon as they set the fire.

*I'm missing something,* I thought over and over and over again.

The doorbell of my apartment chimed. I looked at the clock on the desk in my office. It was almost nine at night. When I reached the front door, I checked out the peephole and saw Shannon shivering out in the cold. My head thumped against the door as I knocked my forehead against it.

"Nathan?" she called out.

I pulled the door open and stepped out of her way. "Hey. What are you doing here? I wasn't expecting you till tomorrow." I wasn't exactly expecting her then either. With everything that had happened since Monday, we'd hardly spoken, much less finalized plans.

"I was worried about you." She put her bag down and unbuttoned her coat. "Your mom said that—"

I cut her off with a wave of my hand. "My mother? You're still talking to my mother?"

She blinked with surprise. "Well, yeah. I emailed her when I didn't hear back from you on Tuesday. She sent me the news article on the girl who died and said she was worried you were taking it really hard."

I bit the insides of my lips to keep my mouth from flying off on its own accord.

She draped her coat over the back of my recliner. "Are you mad?"

I blew out a slow puff of air. "I'm not mad, but I'm not exactly happy either to be honest. I've got a lot of stuff going on and I like you, but..."

Her shoulders sank. "I'm sorry,

Nathan." She picked up her coat again. "I just wanted to help."

As she reached for her bag, I grabbed her arm. "No, I'm sorry. Come here."

God, she smelled good. Like a long winter nap and fresh laundry—both of which I needed desperately. "Is that lavender?" I asked, nuzzling my face against her neck.

She giggled. "You know what lavender is?"

"I have sisters."

"Oh yes. Lara and Karen, correct?" she asked.

Pulling back, I narrowed my eyes. "Geez, how much have you been talking to my mom?"

She put her hands on my chest. "Not too much. She's worried about you. So am I." She batted her eyes up at me. "Can I do anything to make you feel better."

I smiled. I could think of a few things.

I was wide awake well into the middle of the night, despite Shannon's valiant attempt to exhaust me. Absentmindedly, I traced my finger up and down her spine as she lay sprawled out across my mattress in the moonlight. Every time I closed my eyes, I saw

Anthony Withers' face across that lawn. It was the same face I'd had while I watched police search the parking lot after a football game during my senior year of high school. I knew then, just like Anthony did, that I would never see my sister again.

Maybe it was Lieutenant Carr's voice haunting me, but I couldn't shake the feeling that Carissa Withers wouldn't be dead if the robbery cases had my full attention. But how could it? I was also more certain than ever that a serial killer was lurking in North Carolina, and it was only a matter of time before another girl was taken.

I looked down at Shannon, and my heart lurched at the thought that it could be her. What if she was next?

*Good god, I have real feelings for this woman.* I sat up in the darkness of my room and swung my legs off the bed.

"Nathan?" I heard Shannon whisper.

Reaching behind me, I ran my hand along her bare arm. "Shh. Go back to sleep."

I got up and tugged on the gym shorts I had discarded by the bed, then quietly crept out of my room and down the hall to my office. I flipped on the light and flinched as it burned my retinas. For ten solid minutes, I sat with my feet propped up on the desk and stared at the map of North Carolina on the wall.

*Two women in Raleigh, two in Greensboro, two in Hickory, two around Winston-Salem, two around Statesville, and Leslie Ann Bryson in Asheville.*

"Oh shit!" I sat up so fast that I knocked a cup full of pens off my desk.

*How have I not seen this before? If Leslie Bryson was another victim of the same perp, that would make Asheville the only city with only one victim...*

"Is everything OK in here?" Shannon was rubbing her eyes as she walked into the room. "I heard a noise."

"I'm sorry. I knocked some stuff off my desk." Her perfect legs were peeking out from underneath my NC State t-shirt. "Go back to bed, babe. I'll be there in a minute."

She circled her arms around my neck from behind. "What are you doing in here?"

"Working." I pointed to the map. "I think I just figured out something important."

"Oh yeah?" she asked.

I nodded. "Either there's another missing woman in Asheville or there's about to be."

She yawned. "Is it going to happen before breakfast?"

"Uh, I don't think so."

She tugged on my arm. "Then come back to bed with me. You can figure it out tomorrow."

\* \* \*

The next morning, I went for an early run before Shannon woke up, and on my way back to the apartment stopped and got the mail that had been piling up in my mailbox all week long. When I walked back through my front door, I could smell sausage sizzling in the kitchen. Shannon, still wearing nothing but my t-shirt, was standing at the stove.

"Breakfast?" I asked, walking up behind her.

She looked back over her shoulder as I deposited the mail on the counter and slipped my arms around her waist. "I found the sausage in the freezer, but it didn't have a date on it, so I'm praying it doesn't kill us. The only thing else you have to eat here is an alarming amount of candy."

I laughed. "That's why I run." I kissed the bend of her neck as she turned a patty. "I could get used to this."

A small moan escaped her throat. "Do you have to work today?"

I nodded and pulled away from her. "Yeah." I started flipping through the mail on the counter. "And as much as the guys at work would love to meet you, you'll have to stay here."

"I assumed as much. I brought my laptop to keep myself busy," she said.

Underneath my March copy of Maxim magazine was a flyer for Daycon Securities. I picked it up and read it aloud. "Top of the line wireless security, remote web and mobile access, secure remote video monitoring."

She giggled. "You really do need a security system to protect your television and recliner."

I pinched her side. "Shut up." Leaning against the counter, I tapped the flyer against my forehead. Dots were desperately trying to connect in my brain when it hit me. "Remote web access."

"What?" she asked.

Excited, I kissed her cheek. "I swear I think better when you're here."

She held up a piece of sausage to my lips. "I'll take that as a compliment."

I bit into it and smiled. "I'm going to go take a shower."

"Need some help?"

I laughed as I backed out of the kitchen. "Woman, I'll never get to work!"

# NINE

IF I WERE a skipping kind of guy, I would have skipped into the office that morning.

Margaret noticed my chipperness and lowered her reading glasses to look at me. "Morning, Detective."

I slapped my palm down on the surface of her desk. "Good morning, Marge! Glorious day, isn't it?"

Her right eyebrow peaked. "You're making me nervous."

I rubbed my palms together. "It's going to be a good day. I can feel it!"

"Good luck with that," she said, chuckling to herself.

"Marge, have you seen Detective Reese yet this morning?" I asked.

She shook her head. "Not yet. Want me to try and get ahold of him for you?"

I knocked my knuckles against the table top before stepping toward the office door. "Nah, I'll take care of it. Have a great day."

She went back to pecking away on her computer keyboard. "You too, Nathan."

The office was quieter than usual, but it was Friday, so that wasn't a surprise. Lieutenant Carr's office door was closed, and his light was off. I silently thanked God for small blessings. As I walked to my office, I pulled out my cell phone and called Reese.

"Yo," he answered.

"Where are you?"

"Pulling in the lot," he said.

I stuck my key into my door. "Awesome. Meet me in my office."

"10-4." The line went dead.

Turning on the light as I entered, I dropped my stuff on my desk and flipped on my desktop computer. As it booted, I picked up the office phone and punched in the extension for the jail on the back of the property.

"Master control," a man answered.

"This is Detective McNamara. I need inmate trustee Dennis Morgan sent to my office as soon as someone can escort him over," I said.

"Roger that, Detective," he said.

I cradled the receiver just as Reese walked through my door, shaking his head as he crossed the room. "You're way too productive too early this morning." He flopped down in one of my arm chairs. "What's going on."

"I think I know how they're doing it," I said.

He crossed his arms over his chest. "Enlighten me."

I handed him the flyer I'd received in the mail. "Don't you find it curious that the thieves magically know who keeps cash in their safes?"

He nodded. "Of course."

I leaned back in my chair. "I mean, you wouldn't think too many people would keep loads of cash at home, right?"

"Right."

I pointed at him. "I'm willing to bet that each one of these houses has a security camera trained on the safe. I know I've seen at least a couple of them," I said. "ArmorTech offers remote video access. I guarantee you someone is hacking that system and watching that video."

Reese's eyes widened. "And shutting down the system before they go in."

I smiled. "Bingo."

"Well, shit." He handed the flyer back to me. "How are you going to prove it?"

"I'm going to consult with a criminal."

He laughed. "Oh, really?"

"Yep."

"What do you need me to do?"

I jerked my thumb toward the computer monitor. "Can you find those surveillance clips for me? And do some digging to find out if ArmorTech has ever been hacked before?"

He nodded and stood up. "Yeah."

"Hey, Reese?"

He turned back around.

"But be chill about it. It could be someone on the inside over there for all we know."

He smirked. "When am I ever anything but chill?"

I laughed. "Thanks, man."

As he walked out, Dennis Morgan—dressed in orange and white stripes—walked in. "You asked to see me, Detective?"

"Yes." I nodded toward the chairs. "Have a seat, please."

Obediently, Dennis dropped into a chair. "What'cha need?"

Leaning forward, I rested my elbows on my desk. "I need some information. Techie stuff."

One of his flaming red eyebrows arched in question. I was about to be in his debt, and he knew it. "Information, huh?"

I nodded. "You know I can't get any time knocked off your sentence. You've only got a few weeks left," I explained. "But how about a meal from the outside or something?"

"How about The Walking Dead?"

I turned my ear toward him. "Excuse me?"

He smiled. "Man, I haven't seen anything since the mid-season finale last year. You know, Rick shot that little Sophia girl on the farm. She was a zombie and shit." He shook his head sadly. "I don't know. I think the group might turn on him or something."

*That was a good episode.*

"You want to watch The Walking Dead?" I asked to clarify.

"Yeah."

Shaking my head, I laughed. Hard. "That's the most interesting request I've ever received."

"So, is it a deal?" he asked.

"It's a deal. If you can help me."

He sat up straight. "All right. Hit me with it. What do you need?"

"You're in for hacking, right?" I asked.

"Yeah."

"How possible is it to hack into a home security system? One that's web-based, online."

He laughed. "For you?"

I pointed at him. "No. For someone like you."

"Pshhh..." He sat back in his seat again. "Piece of cake." Then, as if remembering his stripes and current incarceration, he began cautiously searching the corners of the ceiling for bugs. "I mean... I've never done that or anything."

Chuckling to myself, I held up a hand to silence him. "No one's listening."

He seemed to relax a bit.

The truth was, Dennis wasn't a bad guy. He'd hacked the computer at the hospital and erased the debts of cancer patients. I'm not saying I would've let him go—a crime is a crime and it's my job to enforce the law—but there's a big difference between Dennis and whoever shot Carissa Withers.

He leaned toward me and lowered his voice. "Give me enough time and I can get into the Pentagon." He looked around cautiously. "What do you need?"

*Man, he must really want to watch some zombies.*

I held up my hand again. "That's not necessary." I handed him the flyer for Daycon. "I'm curious about something like this."

He laughed and didn't even accept the flier. "Shit, man. Daycon has holes in it like swiss cheese. My niece could get through their shit and she's seven."

"Really?"

"Yeah. You can get through their net with a decent SDR and a—"

I cut him off. "A what?"

"SDR," he said again. "Software-defined radio. It lets you intercept and monitor transmissions from shit like Daycon's systems."

"How easy is it to get ahold of?" I asked.

He shrugged. "You got an eBay account?"

*God, I love it when I'm right.*

"So, if they had video surveillance inside the home?" I asked, leading him with my tone.

He laughed and winked a light brown eye at me. "If they've got inside surveillance, then pray they've got hot chicks and those cameras turned toward the showers, dude."

By the end of the day, I was more certain than ever that a hacker was responsible for, or at least involved in, the robberies. All of the video footage that Reese was able to pull had clear footage of the safes, so whoever it was knew the contents of each safe that was hit. I was also willing to bet that whoever Justin Sider was had watched the mayor use his handy-dandy password notebook to access his accounts.

Before I could leave for the day, there was one more order of business I had to tend to. I picked up the phone in my office and dialed our IT department.

"Ramon?" I asked through the intercom.

"Yeah?"

"Can you do me a favor?"

There was a beat of silence. "Sure, Nate. What's up?"

"Can you find a way to buy, download, stream, or whatever all the episodes for last few months of The Walking Dead?" I asked.

"Um…" There was more silence on his end of the phone. "Sure, I guess."

"Great." I stood up at my desk. "Make sure it gets sent over to the jail. They are expecting it. Tell them it's for inmate Dennis Morgan, from me."

"Uh, OK."

"Thanks, Ramon," I said. "Have a good weekend."

"You too, Detective."

I pressed a few buttons to forward my calls to voicemail, then shut down my computer. It was time to head home for the weekend…home to my girlfriend.

# TEN

PERHAPS I SHOULD'VE felt the disruption in the atmosphere when I pulled into the parking lot of my apartment complex, but I didn't sense how off the universe was until I opened my front door and was hit in the face by the scent of pine cleaner and lemon dusting crap. I almost backed quietly out and ran for the hills without a word, but Shannon appeared from the kitchen as soon as I walked in.

She clapped her hands together with glee. "You're home!"

Things were sparkling. I didn't like it. This wasn't home. This was a trap. A domestic trap. I shoved my keys into my pocket and looked around suspiciously like toxic gases might start flooding from the vents.

"What did you do?"

"I just straightened up a bit," she said as she sashayed toward me.

I unzipped my coat. "I…um…it looks ___"

She cut me off by grabbing the lapel of my jacket. "Leave the coat on," she said. "We've got to get going."

"Get going where?" I asked.

"Your parents'."

"Excuse me?"

She giggled and leaned into me. "We're having dinner at your parents' house tonight instead of tomorrow."

Surely, I misheard her. Or misunderstood. Or suffered a stroke between my truck and the front door. "What?"

"Remember? Your mother and I set it up a few days ago. She's cooking and I promised to bring dessert."

*Shit.* I had completely forgotten all about it. Warning bells were chiming in my brain. Red flags were waving before my eyes. "Shannon, don't you think it's a little soon to be meeting my parents?"

She draped her arms around my neck. Her perfume was intoxicating.

*Keep your head, Nate. This is how she sucks you in every damn time.*

"Do you think it's too soon?" She moved so close that her breasts brushed against my chest.

My eyes closed involuntarily. I felt my head shaking 'no' despite the screams of the dying bachelor inside me.

I've never been afraid of commitment; I've just never had time for it. And something about this chick made me feel like I wasn't behind the wheel of this love boat, and I didn't like that one bit. In fact, I was pretty sure I was playing scalawag to Shannon at the helm and my mother as first mate.

Her lips trailed soft kisses down the side of my neck.

I had to remind myself to breathe.

"How long does it take to get to their house?"

"Huh?"

She pulled back. "Nathan."

I opened my eyes and realized my head had dropped back toward the ceiling and my mouth was hanging open. I blinked. "Sorry, what?"

"How long does it take to get to their

- 113 -

house?"

I sighed. "About forty-five minutes."

She dug her fingers into my hips. "Well, we'd better get going so we're not late." She leaned close to my ear. "And because the sooner we get there, the sooner we can get back home."

I whimpered. I actually whimpered.

And before I could object any further, we were on our way to see my parents.

\* \* \*

As my luck would have it, my mother had turned dinner into a family affair. Lara's van was in the driveway, and my brother Chuck's truck was parked near the barn. Chuck lived ten hours away. I prayed that his presence was a coincidence.

I saw the curtains in the formal living room flutter as we walked up the steps. There was no doubt in my mind that my mother had been perched at that window like a kid waiting on Santa. The front door flew open and she sailed out onto the porch with her arms stretched wide.

"You made it!" she cheered.

My father was standing behind Mom with his hands stuffed into his pockets and a look in his eyes that said he had nothing to do with it. I kissed Mom's cheek. "Hello, Mother." I stepped to her side. "Mom, this is Shannon."

"Oh!" Mom stepped forward to greet her with a hug. "It's so nice to finally meet you, dear!"

*Finally? It's been like three weeks!*

I leaned toward my dad. "She's killing me," I whispered.

He winked. "Which one?"

We both laughed.

"I brought pie," Shannon said, holding out the dish we'd picked up at the supermarket on the way. "I would have baked something myself, but Nathan's kitchen isn't exactly equipped."

Rolling my eyes, I looked at Dad. "I have a can opener and a frying pan. What more do I need?"

Shannon giggled and looped her arm through mine.

"I'm sure this will be wonderful," Mom said, taking it from her. "Come on in out of the cold, you two."

Once we were inside, loud squeals erupted down the hallway. The family door nearly flew off its hinges and smacked back against the wall as Carter tore down the hallway wearing Spiderman pajamas, a Batman mask, and ginormous green Hulk fists on his hands.

"Unca Nate!"

I laughed and caught him around the middle as he charged me. As I draped him over my shoulder, I looked at Shannon. "Shannon, this is my nephew, Iron Man."

He kicked his legs. "I not I-won Man!"

"Oh, I'm sorry!" I smacked myself in the forehead. "I mean Superman."

"I Spida-man, Unca Nate!"

"I think you're confused," I said, carrying him down the hallway.

He was still flailing over my shoulder. "No, I not!"

Shannon practically had cartoon hearts bulging from her eyeballs. I put Carter down and he took off running again. She slipped her fingers between mine.

"Go on into the living room," Mom said behind us. "Your brother's here."

I pushed the swinging door to the family room open and let Shannon go in first. My brother, Chuck, stood when we entered.

Lara was beside him. Chuck looked like a lumberjack compared to the rest of us. He had a thick brown beard and was, like usual, wearing camo. By comparison, I was short, scrawny, and blond but so was everyone else in the McNamara clan. So if anyone was adopted, we all knew who it was.

"Hey, little brother," Chuck said, closing his arms around me. "How the hell are ya?" He thumped me so hard on the back, it triggered a cough.

"I'm good, old man. What are you doing here?" I stepped back and looked up at him.

He nodded toward Dad. "We're going to the game this weekend."

Tossing my hands up, I looked at our father. "Seriously, I'm never invited!"

Dad shrugged. "You're always working. I asked you to go weeks ago."

He probably did and I didn't remember. Nevertheless, I shook my head. "Whatever."

Chuck squeezed my shoulder. "I got you a present." He reached into his pocket and pulled out a small fabric rectangle. "It's for your hat." He flicked the brim of my ball cap.

I looked down at the velcro patch. It had a picture of an assault rifle on it and it said, 'I Plead the Second'. I laughed. "That's pretty funny." I showed it to Dad.

Lara cleared her throat. "Nathan, aren't you going to introduce your friend?"

"Oh, sorry!" I turned toward Shannon. "Shannon, this is my sister, Lara, and my brother, Chuck. You met Carter when we came in and"—I looked around the room —"where's Rachel?"

"Rachel has dance tonight." Lara offered Shannon her hand. "It's nice to meet you." Lara's tone was warm and kind, but she was taking a close inventory of Shannon who was wearing a casual gray dress and heels opposed to my sister's yoga pants and Wolfpack sweatshirt.

"Thanks! You too!" Shannon chirped a little too eagerly.

Chuck caught my eye and mouthed the word 'wow' as he gave a discreet thumbs-up.

Mom held up her hands to get our attention. "Shall we eat before dinner gets cold?"

Chuck rubbed his hands together. "I'm starving!"

Mom looked at Lara. "Or should we wait on Joe?"

Lara checked her watch. "No, let's go ahead and eat. I'll save him a plate."

Gently, I touched the small of Shannon's back and nudged her toward the dining room door. I looked back at my mother. "Dining room, Mom?"

She nodded. "Of course."

"Oh, the grown-ups' table." Chuck laughed. "This must be a very special occasion."

Shannon looked over her shoulder at me. "The grown-ups table?"

We all filed into the formal dining room. The table was set with the good china. I stopped at the chair next to mine and pulled it out for Shannon. "When we were kids and Mom threw dinner parties, this was always the grown-ups table and all us kids had to eat in the kitchen."

Chuck pulled out his chair. "Even as adults, we never eat in here except on Thanksgiving or Christmas." He winked at her. "You must be a very big deal."

Dad sat down at the head of the table. "It's not every day that Nathan brings a lady home."

"Or any day," Lara said, helping Carter into his booster seat.

I threw a cloth napkin across the table at her.

Mom clapped her hands together angrily. "Stop it, you two! This is exactly why you still have to eat in the kitchen!"

Everyone laughed.

The meal was fit for a holiday: honey glazed ham, scalloped potatoes, broccoli casserole, homemade rolls, fruit salad, and even though Shannon was supposed to bring dessert, Mom baked a cream cheese pound cake.

"You've really done too much," Shannon said, her nerves still causing her voice to be way too chipper. "I hope you didn't go to too much trouble for me."

My mother waved her hand toward Shannon. "This is nothing, my dear. We have family dinners quite often." She reached over and squeezed my dad's hand. "We're very close like that."

Shannon smiled at me. "Well, I hope

this won't be my last invitation."

I wasn't sure why she was looking at me; I didn't invite her, period.

Lara might have been reading my mind across the table because when I looked at her, her eyes were as wide as mine felt.

"So, Shannon," Chuck said with a mouthful of potatoes. "What do you do?"

She put her napkin beside her plate. "I'm a reporter for WKNC in Asheville."

He nodded, impressed.

Shannon was fidgeting. "My daddy wanted me to go into banking like he did. He's one of the biggest investment bankers in Asheville."

Well, that was random. And awkward.

Mom and Dad exchanged glances. "Well, that's lovely," Mom finally said. "What about your mother. Does she work?"

"Not exactly." She shifted on her chair. "But she does organize the Ladies' Social Auxiliary at the Brook Diamond Country Club."

Mom stopped chewing. The only social club she'd ever belonged to was the PTO.

Shannon flipped her blond hair back

off her shoulder. "And she manages the household staff."

*Staff?* I could hear the sound of a plane crashing in my head.

Chuck plucked a stray piece of ham from his beard. "I hired the neighbor's kid to cut my grass during squirrel season last summer."

The room erupted in laughter.

"You hunt squirrels?" Shannon asked.

I leaned toward her. "He hunts anything with fur or feathers."

Her nose scrunched up. "Do you eat them?"

He smiled. "Sometimes."

She visibly shuddered.

Lara kicked me in the shin under the table, and I flinched.

"Unca Chuck said I can eat da sqwa-wills bwains!" Carter chimed in.

Chuck pointed his fork at him. "Only if you skin it, remember?"

Mom shook her head. "Enough of that talk at the table!" She dropped her hands into her lap. "I swear you all don't know how to behave when we have company."

Chuck pointed at Carter. "He brought

up the brains."

I covered my mouth to keep from laughing.

"Charles Mason McNamara!" Mom scolded.

He just shrugged and shoved a forkful of ham into his mouth.

I leaned into Shannon. "I should've warned you about my family."

She smiled and dabbed her napkin on her lips. "I like them."

Looking around the table, I wasn't sure if they would say the same.

Deciding to change the subject, I looked at Dad. "So about this game...are they playing UNC at home this weekend?"

Chuck rolled his eyes. "Would I have driven all the way from Tennessee for any other game?"

I slammed my napkin down on the table. "Damn it."

"Nathan! Carter's here. Watch your mouth!" Mom yelled.

"Damn it," Carter echoed, then burst into giggles.

Lara clamped her hand over his mouth and shot me a hateful glare.

I held up my hands. "Sorry." I leaned an elbow on the table. "I wonder how much scalped tickets are going for."

Lara smirked. "You're going to buy illegally scalped basketball tickets, Mr. Law Enforcement Officer?"

I shrugged and sat back in my chair. "It's the biggest game of the season."

No one argued.

Mom cleared her throat. "Nathan, are you forgetting about your houseguest?"

*Oops.*

I looked at Shannon. "Do you like basketball?"

She smiled. "I'd love to go to the game!"

*Well, that's a point in her favor.*

Then she spoke again.

"I really hope the Tarheels make it to the championship!"

And that was all she wrote for Shannon Green.

# ELEVEN

FOR THE REST of my weekend with Shannon, I was flooded with phone calls from my mother, my sister, and even Chuck. Lara was the least delicate of the bunch, threatening my life if I married Shannon or accidentally got her pregnant. Mom was polite, but she apologized for forcing the family dinner so quickly. And Chuck…well, his response was 'If it doesn't work out, send her my way. She's hot and I'm sure she can make a sandwich.' He's a classy dude, my brother.

We didn't go to the game either. I didn't even get to watch it on television because Shannon wanted to go see some romantic comedy with that blond chick from Grey's Anatomy, whose last name looks like a vagina exercise. It was an excellent way to spend a Saturday. Right.

Shannon left early on Sunday and I watched the game on DVR. But because I have a police scanner, I already knew who won. It wasn't nearly as much fun watching, knowing State lost 63 to 54.

And before I knew it, Monday arrived and I was pulling back into my parking space at the sheriff's office—at the exact same time as the lieutenant. I muttered a few explicatives before getting out of my SUV.

"Good morning, Lieutenant." I carried my hazelnut coffee around his car. "Did you have a nice weekend?"

"Reese said that you made a connection with the break-ins." He slammed his driver's side door. "Why wasn't I briefed on it?"

The muscle worked in my jaw as I tried to calm my temper. "You were out on Friday, sir."

"I have a phone."

I nodded and fell in step behind him. "Yes, but there was no reason to bother you on your day off, so I decided to wait until first thing this morning."

# THE DETECTIVE

He spun on his heel toward me. "Detective, you're on thin ice with me as it is. I don't think you're pulling your weight on this case. So I suggest that any time you have even the smallest crumb of information, you pass it along to me directly." Droplets of spit sprayed my sunglasses. "Your job depends on it!"

Frozen to the ground, I watched as he stormed inside the building. What I had done to make him hate me so much, I wasn't sure. This conversation confirmed it though; Carr was gunning for my job. After a moment, I trudged inside after him.

Marge looked worried. "You all right?"

"You heard that?"

She just nodded.

I forced a smile. "I'm fine. How was your weekend?"

"The grandbaby shoved seven rolls of toilet paper down the toilet, then flushed it." She looked at me and frowned. "He's a little less cute now."

I laughed. "Have a good day, Marge."

"You too, Detective." She smiled. "Keep your chin up."

Sucking in a deep breath, I pushed the office door open and walked in like I hadn't just been verbally kicked in the nuts outside. When I went into my office, I shut the door behind me, but by the time I'd made it around to my desk Reese had reopened it and walked in.

"Morning, sunshine," he said.

"Ugh."

He sat down across from me. "That good, huh?"

I relayed the conversation with our boss.

When I was finished, he shook his head. "What's the deal with you two? Did you screw his daughter or something?"

I tossed my hands up. "I don't freaking know!"

He folded his hands behind his head. "There's got to be a reason."

I rolled my eyes. "Well, I hope I figure it out before he fires me."

Reese smirked. "He's not going to fire you."

"Easy for you to say." I turned on my computer. "Please tell me there wasn't another break-in over the weekend."

He shook his head. "Quiet as church."

"That's good." I tapped a pen against my desk. "I doubt there will be any more."

"Really?"

I nodded. "Yeah. They upped the ante to homicide now. They're scared."

He blew out a slow breath. "I hope you're right. So you think they were just after the cash?"

The question made me think. "I don't know if it was just the money or the thrill of getting away with it too. You should've seen how Morgan lit up the other day, telling me about what he could pull off as a hacker."

He grinned. "Think it's Morgan?"

I laughed. "That would be impressive." I pulled out a pad of sticky notes. "I need to remember to go check and make sure he got his zombie shows this weekend." In all caps, I wrote 'SEE DENNIS MORGAN' and stuck it to the top of my computer screen.

My office phone beeped, and Marge's voice came over the loudspeaker. "Detective McNamara, the State Crime Lab is on line four."

"Thanks, Marge. Put 'em through." I

looked at Reese. "Cross your fingers." I pressed the blinking line four button on my phone and left the speaker on. "Detective McNamara," I said.

Reese got up and closed my office door.

"Good morning, Detective," a woman said. "My name is Deborah Jacobs at the State Crime Lab. We met last year on the Hilton murder case."

My brain churned on her name. Deborah Jacobs—brunette, mid-forties, double-D's. "Hi, Deborah. I remember you. What can I do for you?"

"I wanted to let you know that we were able to pull a fingerprint off your murder weapon."

I bolted upright in my seat. "Oh, really?"

Reese leaned over my desk toward the phone.

"We lifted a right thumb print off the barrel. And we have a match for it."

I stood so quickly, I knocked over my office chair. "Who is it?"

"I'm sending over the info now, but his name is Kyle Anthony Culver. Twenty-seven, lives in Millbrook." Papers rustled on her end of the line. "He was fingerprinted during a college internship for a weapons vulnerability software company in Raleigh."

I slammed my palms down on the desk. "Bingo."

Reese backed toward the door. "I'll get the DA on the phone."

"Thank you, Deborah. I owe you my first-born," I said.

She chuckled. "Not necessary. Check your email."

After disconnecting the call, I downloaded her report to my computer and printed two copies. One of them, I carried straight to Carr's office. The door was closed, but I walked in anyway. The sheriff was sitting in front of his desk, but I didn't care.

The lieutenant's face flushed red with anger. "McNamara, what makes you think you can just barge in here—"

I cut him off by slamming the report down on his desk with the full force of my hand. "There's your shooter, Lieutenant."

The sheriff stood and leaned over the desk. "The Withers girl's murderer?"

I looked down at him. "Exactly. The

State Crime Lab just called."

Sheriff Tipper slapped me on the back. "Good work, son."

"Reese is getting started with the warrant, sir." I lowered my head so I was eye-level with him. "I may need you to make a phone call to help push this through, so I can go get this guy immediately."

He nodded. "Of course I will. Go get him."

I smiled, my heart pounding with excitement. "10-4, sir."

\* \* \*

Within the hour, I had a signed arrest warrant in my hand. In all my years at the department, I'd never seen the wheels of justice turn so fast. Reese and I were escorted in his unmarked sedan by two deputies in patrol cars, and on our drive to Millbrook, Shannon called.

I held the phone to my ear. "Hey, babe."

"Hey," she said. "How's your Monday?"

"Amazing. We finally have a solid lead on that case I'm working on."

"That's wonderful, Nathan." She paused for a beat. "Unless you're joking and then it's not funny at all."

I pulled the phone away from my head and stared at it for a second. "Joking?" I finally asked her. "Why would I joke about something like this?"

"Because it's April Fools' Day," she said.

I looked at the date on my watch. It was April 1st. I had no idea. "No. I'm definitely not joking. We're on our way to make an arrest right now."

"Oh, well that's good. Our office has been rampant with pranks today. Our IT guy had a sign made that said our office printer was now upgraded to use voice recognition software. I stood there yelling at the printer to print for ten minutes before they finally clued me in."

I covered my mouth, but chuckled anyway. "I'm sorry. That's pretty funny."

She let out a huff. "I swear those computer guys have way too much power."

I was still laughing at the thought of her talking to the printer when Reese slapped me on the arm and pointed to the street sign where Culver's apartment building was. "Shannon, I've got to go. We're almost there. I'll call you later."

"Good luck!" she said before I disconnected the line.

I looked at Reese. "Did you remember it's April Fools' Day?"

He nodded. "I was gonna tell you that Carr told someone you were getting canned, but after your story this morning, I worried it might be true."

I slugged him in the arm as he turned into the apartment complex.

Through the windshield, I studied the building. "I hope this isn't a prank."

"I'll kill somebody myself if it is," Reese said and put the car in park.

The front door of the apartment was standing open, so we walked in with guns drawn. The television was on and water was boiling on the stove next to a box of macaroni. But no one was home. Kyle Culvers had left in a hurry.

I holstered my Glock. "It's like the bastard knew we were coming!"

Reese looked at me. "He had to know. But how?"

Shaking my head, I looked around the apartment. "I need to think."

Reese smirked. "Good luck with that."

I held up my middle finger. "Don't touch anything," I told the other two deputies. "Reese, go check his closet. I'll bet he's a size ten."

He nodded and walked down the hallway. I pulled out my cell phone and began making calls. The first was to put out an APB on the car Culvers was driving. Judging by the amount of water left in the boiling pot on the stove, I guessed he didn't have that much of a head start. The second call I made was to the sheriff, so he would hear the bad news from me instead of Carr. I called Carr last, but hung up in the middle of his rant when Reese reappeared with a pair of sneakers dangling from his fingertips.

"Size ten. You called it," he said.

A deputy produced an evidence bag.

I shoved my phone in my pocket. "We need to get back to the office so I can figure out if we've got a mole or not."

Reese's eyebrows lifted. "You think it's someone on our side?"

We walked outside and I turned

toward the deputies. "Secure this place and sit on it. I want statements from all the neighbors. I'll be back." I looked at Reese. "You got a better idea?"

He pulled out his key fob and unlocked his car. "The State knew, so did countless people at the courthouse."

I opened the passenger's side door and looked at him over the roof. "Yeah, but it's too coincidental that all of our officers have been just far enough away for the perps to escape each crime scene. Now this."

He nodded as we got in the car. "Good point."

I leaned against the door and tugged my ball cap down tight over my eyes. "But how?"

When I sat up and looked toward Reese again, my eyes fell to the laptop mounted on his dash. "Holy shit."

He slammed on his brakes mid-way through backing out of his space. "What?"

I slammed his laptop shut as I repeated Shannon's words. "The computer guys have too much power."

His eyes doubled in size. "Ramon."

"Get to the office, *now*!"

# TWELVE

USING MY PERSONAL phone, I called the lieutenant directly and explained the situation. At first he laughed at me, reasoning that no one in *his* office could possibly be dirty right under his nose. But after a moment of likely considering the consequences for his career should I be right and he be wrong, he consented to put the office on lockdown.

"Is he going to wait for us to get there?" Reese asked as he sped down the interstate.

I laughed but didn't think it was funny. "I doubt it."

"So he can take all the glory, I'm sure."

I braced myself against the dash as we took a particularly fast curve off the exit ramp. "I'm sure."

When we peeled into the parking lot a few minutes later, there were several officers outside the main door on the steps. They looked confused and anxious and glad to see two detectives who might know what was going on.

I pulled out my radio. "What's happening in there?" I asked one of the deputies.

He shook his head. "We don't know. The building's on lockdown. Doors are barred and nobody's answering the radio. Somebody said it's something internal."

Cupping my hands around my eyes, I tried to peer through the reflective glass on the front entrance. It was hard to focus through the dim window, but after a second, I registered that Ramon had Marge in his arms, using her as a shield against the deputies with their guns drawn on him in the lobby. Something sharp was in his hand and pointed at her head—or her neck— I couldn't tell.

"What is it?" Reese asked, stepping up behind me.

"He's taken Marge as a hostage!" I spun around. "Everyone get away from the door!"

Reese grabbed my arm. "What are you going to do?"

I aimed my Glock at the door handle. "I'm going to let him out."

"Nate, man, no! That's against protocol—"

"Screw protocol, Reese!" I shouted. "He's going to come through that door and we're going to take him down! He doesn't have a gun and he doesn't know what the hell he's doing."

He was shaking his head. "This is a bad idea, man."

I narrowed my gaze at him. "Trust me."

After a second of deliberating, he took a step back, and I fired off a round at the door where I knew the locking mechanism was housed. The blast was deafening. Just as I predicted, the door swung open and Ramon stumbled back out of it with Marge still in his grip. Reese and I rushed him from both sides, me pushing Marge out of the way and Reese tackling him onto the concrete. Marge's silver letter opener clanged to the ground as it flew from Ramon's grasp.

Reese sat up with his knees still pinning Ramon down on the sidewalk and panting as he pressed Ramon's face into the concrete. "Got him."

I pulled back from where I was sheltering Marge. "Are you OK?"

She had a bloody scratch on her neck and she was visibly trembling, but she nodded. "I'm OK. Thank you, Nathan."

Every other officer inside the jail poured out through the door with their guns aimed at us. I wiped sweat from my brow under my hat. "Show's over, boys."

Carr stormed outside. "I should have known!" he roared.

I rolled off of Marge and onto my ass, still trying to catch my breath. I looked up at him. "It's over."

In two strides, he was almost on top of me. "You just violated about nineteen different—"

"Carr!" I shouted to cut him off.

He stopped, taken back by my tone.

I looked up at him. "Just shut up!"

All eyes in front of the jail went wide. Reese laughed. A few people stumbled back. I didn't care.

Dusting myself off, I stood up and shook my head. "I knew we could take him down and we did. It's over. Punish me. Fire me." I shook my head. "I don't even care anymore." I offered Marge my hand and helped her to her feet. Another officer took her under his arm and led her back toward the building. I stopped just in front of my boss's face. "Excuse me. I've got work to do."

# THIRTEEN

CARR DIDN'T FIRE me, but only because he couldn't afford to and keep his job. By the end of the day, the story had reached the local news. By the weekend, it had gone national. The sheriff's job is a political office and it was an election year, so I smiled for the cameras, knowing each headline meant job security.

Ramon Edgar had been the inside-man pumping information about the sheriff's office to his two friends, Kyle Culvers and Travis Bell—a.k.a. Justin Sider. Travis, an M.I.T. engineering drop-out, had been the ring leader of the trio and was an expert at cracking safes. He had once even taught a seminar on it at an international security conference. Just as I suspected, they were targeting homes protected by ArmorTech. They had spent months driving around nice neighborhoods looking for ArmorTech stickers on houses and then had hacked into the video feeds of each one. When they found a house with a large stash of cash, they planned their attack, waiting till no one was home, then disabling each system remotely prior to going in.

The death of Carissa Withers was a tragic miscalculation on their part. Still, Kyle Culvers, the trigger man, went up for second degree murder and the other two were charged with everything from accessory to tampering with evidence. All three of them would spend the majority of the rest of their lives in federal prison.

As far as I could tell, none of them had any grand plans for their loot aside from buying computer equipment and video game add-ons. Ramon had reportedly purchased a $6,000 elf on World of Warcraft through an auction in Australia. When I found out, I suddenly felt better about my non-existent social life.

Speaking of…

I spent the weekend dodging the

media in Asheville.

On Friday night, Shannon took me downtown to eat dinner. Tupelo Honey was packed with a line of people waiting to get in, but she swore it was some of the best food in town and well worth the wait. When we were finally taken to our table, a surprising face was at the table next to ours.

"Sheriff Davis," I said, putting my hand on his shoulder.

He looked up, then smiled when he saw me and stood. He offered me his hand. "Detective McNamara. Fancy meetin' you here. How are ya?"

I nodded. "I've been busy."

He laughed. "So I've heard." He pumped my fist again. "Congratulations on the robbery case. You've been all over the news, even here."

I blew out a sigh. "Between you and me, I'm just glad it's over. That was months of headache and frustration."

"It usually is," he said. "What brings you back to town?"

I looked over at Shannon. "Asheville hospitality."

He chuckled and waved to her. "Nice

to see you again, Ms. Green." He looked down at the woman sitting next to him. "This is my wife, Gloria. Gloria, this is the hotshot investigator from Raleigh I've been trying to get moved out here, Nathan McNamara."

I tipped my hat in her direction. "Nice to meet you, ma'am."

She smiled politely.

He crossed his large arms over his chest. "Have you thought anymore about my offer?"

I laughed. "Honestly, sir, I've been so busy, I haven't had time to think about anything."

He pointed at me. "Well, don't forget about it, son."

I smiled and shook my head. "I won't." I bowed my head slightly. "I hope you enjoy your dinner."

He nodded. "And you as well."

Just as I joined Shannon at our table, my cell phone buzzed in my pocket. I pulled it out and looked at the screen. It was the lieutenant. I groaned and looked at Shannon. "Babe, will you excuse me for just a sec? I've got to take this. It's my boss."

She smiled. "Want me to order a drink

for you?"

I glanced back at the bar. "Yeah, a pale ale on tap."

She nodded as I walked away and pressed the answer button on my phone. I held it to my ear as I stepped back outside in the cold. "McNamara."

"Nathan, I'm going to need you out with Wallace on the double homicide in Rolesville tonight," Carr said in lieu of a greeting.

I rolled my eyes up toward the starry sky. "Lieutenant, I'm not on duty tonight."

"I didn't ask if you were. I said, I need you in Rolesville."

"I'm out of town, sir."

He paused. "I don't believe you cleared your absence with me."

"I'm not on duty," I repeated, over-enunciating my words. "I'm sorry, sir. You're going to have to call someone else."

He began spouting off on the other end of the line, but I wasn't listening. I held the phone away from my mouth and began making static noises. "I'm sorry, Lieutenant. Bad reception. You're breaking up on me."

Then, with a little too much

satisfaction, I pressed the end-call button and powered the phone all the way down before tucking it into my jacket pocket. *Screw that guy.*

With a new quickness to my step, I turned back toward the restaurant just as two women stopped at the front door. They were about my age and both attractive. One was blond and about six feet tall; the other was brunette and a little shorter than me.

"Adrianne, it's packed," the brunette said as she scrunched up her nose.

*God, she's hot.*

The blonde looped her arm through her friend's. "You're right. Let's go grab margaritas instead!"

My feet seemed rooted to the ground, as the brunette glanced over her shoulder at me and smiled. Her eyes were the color of new copper pennies. She looked back at her friend. "Go on then, you're blocking the door!"

My breath hung in my chest as the pair took off down the street toward the sounds of a mariachi band. And like with the force of gravity pulling at me, I wanted to follow.

# THANK YOU FOR READING!

★★★★★

Please consider leaving a review on Amazon!
Reviews help other readers discover new
books.

*Detective Nathan McNamara is one of the
leading men in The Soul Summoner Series.
Turn the page for a free peek at Chapter One.*

The Soul Summoner is a #1 Bestselling
Series on Amazon.

# THE SOUL SUMMONER
## CHAPTER ONE

Her hazel eyes were judging me again. *God, I wish I could read minds instead.*

Adrianne spun her fork into her spaghetti, letting the tines scrape against the china. I cringed from the sound. She pointed her forkful of noodles at my face. "I think you're a witch."

I laughed to cover my nerves. "You've said that before." Under the white tablecloth, I crossed my fingers and prayed we would breeze through this conversation one more time.

A small, teasing smile played at the corner of her painted lips. "I really think you are."

I shook my head. "I'm not a witch."

She shrugged. "You might be a witch."

I picked up my white wine. "I wish I had a dollar for every time I've heard that. I could pay off my student loans." With one deep gulp, I finished off the glass.

She swallowed the bite in her mouth and leaned toward me. "Come on. I might die if I don't get to see him tonight! Do you really want that kind of guilt on your hands?"

I rolled my eyes. "You're so dramatic."

She placed her fork beside her plate and reached over to squeeze my hand. "Please try."

My shoulders caved. "OK." I shoved my chair back a few inches and crossed my legs on top of my seat. I closed my eyes, shook my long brown hair off my shoulders, and blew out a deep slow breath as I made circular O's with my fingertips. Slowly, my hands floated down till they rested on my knees. I began to moan. "Ohhhhhmmmm…"

Adrianne threw her napkin at me, drawing the attention of the surrounding guests at Alejandro's Italian Bistro. "Be serious!"

I dropped my feet to the floor and laughed as I scooted closer to the table. "*You* be serious," I said. "You know that's not how it works."

She laughed. "You don't even know how it works!" She flattened her palms on the tablecloth. "Here, I'll make it easy. Repeat after me. Billy Stewart, Billy Stewart, Billy Stewart," she chanted.

I groaned and closed my eyes. "Billy Stewart, Billy Stewart, Billy Stewart."

She broke out in giggles and covered her mouth. "You're such a freak!"

I raised an eyebrow. "You call me that a lot."

"You know I'm only joking. Sort of."

Adrianne Marx had been my best friend since the fifth grade, but sometimes I still had trouble deciphering when she was joking and when she was being serious.

I picked up my fork again and pointed it at her. "It's not gonna happen, so don't get too excited."

She let out a deep breath. "I'm not."

I smirked. "Whatever."

Our waiter, who had been the topic of our conversation before Adrianne began gushing about her new crush on Billy Stewart, appeared at our table.

"Can I get you ladies anything else?" His Southern drawl was so smooth I had nicknamed him Elvis over dinner. He was a little older than the two of us, maybe twenty-three, and he had a sweet, genuine smile. His hair was almost black, and his eyes were the color of sparkling sapphires. I had drunk enough water that night to float the Titanic just so I could watch him refill my glass.

I looked at his name tag. "Luke, do I look like a witch?"

His mouth fell open. "Uh, I don't think so?" His response was more of a question than an answer.

Across the table, Adrianne was twisting strands of her auburn ponytail around her finger. I nodded toward Luke. "See, he doesn't think I'm a witch."

Luke lowered his voice and leaned one hand on our table. "You're too pretty to be a witch," he added, with a wink.

I smiled with satisfaction.

Adrianne laughed and pushed her plate away from her. "Don't be fooled, Luke. She has powers you can't even dream of."

He looked down at me and smiled. "Oh really?" He leaned down and lowered his voice. "How about you let me take care of this for you"—he dangled our bill in front of my face —"and later, when I get off, I can hear all about your powers?"

Heat rose in my cheeks as I took the check from his hand, and when I pulled a pen from his waistband apron, his breath caught in his chest. I flashed my best sultry smile up at him and scribbled my name and phone number on the back of the bill. I stood up, letting my hand linger in his as I gave him the check. "I'm in town on a break from college for the weekend, so let me know when you get off."

He smiled and backed away from the table. "I will"—he looked down at the paper—"Sloan."

I took a deep breath to calm the butterflies in my stomach as Adrianne followed me toward the front door. She nudged me with her elbow. "You should win some kind of award for being able to pick up guys," she said as we passed through the small rush of dinner customers coming in.

I shrugged my shoulders and glanced back at her with a mischievous grin. "Maybe it's part of my gift."

"Witch," she muttered.

The icy chill of winter nipped at my face as I pushed the glass door open. When we walked out onto the sidewalk, I stopped so suddenly that Adrianne tripped over my legs and tumbled to the concrete.

Billy Stewart was waiting at a red light in front of the restaurant.

\* \* \*

Adrianne might never have even noticed Billy's official game warden truck at the stoplight had my mouth not been hanging open when she struggled to her feet. She was cursing me under her breath as her eyes followed the direction of my dumbfounded gaze across the dark parking lot. When her eyes landed on the green and gold truck, she fell back a step.

Her fingers, still coated in gravel dust, dug into my arm. "Is that…?"

I turned my horrified eyes to meet hers when traffic started moving again.

Frantically, she waved her finger in the direction of the traffic light. "That was Billy Stewart!" She was so excited that her voice cracked.

"Yeah, it was." Mortification settled over me, and I pressed my eyes closed, hoping to wake from a bad dream. When I focused on Adrianne again, I realized she had taken a pretty nasty fall. Her blue jeans were torn and her right knee was bloody. "Oh geez, I'm so sorry."

She looked at me, her eyes wild with a clear mix of anxiety and amusement. She glanced down at the gash on her knee. "Can you heal me too?" Her question had a touch of maniacal laughter.

I shoved her shoulder. "Shut up." I tugged her toward the restaurant's entrance. "Let's go to the bathroom and get you cleaned up."

Once we were behind the closed door of the ladies room, Adrianne's curious eyes turned toward me again. She hiked her leg up on the counter beside the sink. "What the hell just happened out there?"

I ran some cold water over a paper towel and handed it to her. "I need a drink." I splashed my face with cold water and, for a moment, considered drowning myself in the sink.

She pointed at me as she dabbed the oozing blood off her kneecap. "You and me both, sister. You've got some major explaining to do."

Alejandro's had a small bar near the front door where I had never seen anyone actually sit. When we pulled out two empty bar stools, the slightly balding bartender looked at us like we might be lost. His eyebrows rose in question as he mindlessly polished water spots off of a wine glass.

"I think I'm going to need a Jack and Coke," Adrianne announced.

I held up two fingers. "Make that two."

"IDs?" he asked.

Getting carded was one of the best things about being twenty-one. Any other time, I would have whipped out my finally-legal-identification with a smile plastered on my face. But in that moment, fear of what the next conversation might bring loomed over me like a black storm cloud that was ready to drop a funnel.

I had already learned the hard way not to talk about these things.

People are scared of what they can't comprehend, and the last thing I wanted was for Adrianne to be afraid of me. Despite my unnatural propensity toward popularity, Adrianne was one of the only real friends I had.

I knew the jabs she made about me being a witch were all in jest, but there was a part of her that had been genuinely curious about me since we were kids. Adrianne, above anyone else, had the most cause to be suspicious of the odd 'coincidences' that were happening more and more frequently around me.

Summoning Billy Stewart had been a complete accident. God knows I had tried my whole life to summon all sorts of people—my birth mother and Johnny Depp to name a couple—without any success at all. Sitting next to Adrianne at the bar, I knew from the look in her eyes that seeing Billy at that stoplight solidified to her what I already knew to be true: I was different. Very different.

Swiveling her chair around to face me, she pointed to the dining table we had just vacated. "OK, I was kidding about Billy at dinner. That was some serious David Copperfield shit you just pulled out there, Sloan. Totally creepy."

I groaned and dropped my face into my hands. "I know."

An arm came to rest behind my back, and Luke appeared between our seats with a tantalizing grin that would normally make me swoon. "Did you miss me that much?" he asked.

Adrianne pointed a well-manicured fingernail at him. "Not now, Elvis," she said without taking her eyes off me.

Stunned, Luke took a few steps back.

I offered him an apologetic wink. "We need a minute."

He nodded awkwardly, stuffed his hands into his pockets, and left us alone.

When he was gone, I turned back to Adrianne. "I don't suppose you could be convinced this was all a really big coincidence?"

"Sloan, when we ran into my Gran after you said you needed to pick up some canned green beans from her, that was a coincidence. When we were talking about going to Matt Sheridan's keg party and we ran into him at the beer store, that was a coincidence. When you said you hoped Shannon Green would get syphilis and we saw her walking out of the Health Department, maybe even that was a coincidence." We both laughed.

She tapped her nails against the bar top. "Billy Stewart is supposed to be working on the backside of a mountain right now, Sloan. He shouldn't be anywhere near the city. I was joking and trying to get you to make him magically appear...and then *you did*. That's not a coincidence."

I groaned.

She lowered her voice and leaned into me. "What are you not telling me? Did you make that happen or not?"

It was too late to try and recover with a lie. I had no other choice but to tell her the truth. My legs were shaking under the table and a trickle of sweat ran down my spine. "I'm not a hundred percent certain, but yes. I think so."

She sucked in a deep breath and blew it out slowly. Her eyes were wide and looking everywhere but into mine. "I'm going to be honest. You're kinda freaking me out a little bit right now."

I nodded and pinched the bridge of my nose. "I know. I wish I had a grand explanation, but I've never had anyone explain it to me either."

I felt her hand squeeze mine. "I love you, so let me have it. Tell me everything."

My stomach felt like an elevator free-falling through the shaft. "You're going to think I'm crazy."

"Sloan, I think we bypassed crazy about twenty minutes ago," she said with a genuine chuckle.

The bartender placed our drinks in front of us, and I wrapped my fingers around the short tumbler. Adrianne drained half of her whiskey in one swallow.

I took a deep breath. I let my thoughts roll around for a moment in my head, and I tried to choose my words carefully so I didn't sound as nuts as I felt. Finally, I looked at her and lowered my voice. "You know when you're out and you see someone you really feel like you know, but you can't remember how or who they are?"

She nodded. "Sure."

I paused for a moment. "I feel that way around *everyone*. Like I already know them."

Her face contorted with confusion. She tried to laugh it off without success. "Well, I've always said you've never met a stranger."

I looked at her seriously. "I haven't *ever* met a stranger, Adrianne."

She cleared her throat. "I really don't understand what you're talking about."

Sadly, I didn't understand what I was talking about either.

"I see people I've never met and feel like I've known them forever. I can even just see a picture of someone and know if they are alive or dead and what kind of person they are. I don't know their names or anything specific, but I have a weird sense about them before ever talking to them. It's like I recognize their soul."

She let my words sink in for a moment. "Like the time you told me not to go out with the exchange student in the eleventh grade, and then he date-raped that cheerleader?"

"Yes. I knew he had a lot of evil in him," I said.

"And you get these 'vibes' from everyone?" she asked.

I nodded. "Absolutely everyone."

"So that's why you're so good with people...why you can talk to anyone and everyone at any time?"

I nodded again. "It's easy to befriend people when it feels like you've known them for years, and I seem to be somewhat of a people-magnet."

She interrupted me. "But what does that have to do with Billy Stewart showing up here tonight?"

"There's more."

She sat back, exasperated. "Of course there is."

"I think it's somehow related. People are naturally drawn to me, and somehow I can manipulate that."

Her eyes widened. "You can control people?" Her voice was almost a whisper.

"I don't think I would call it *controlling* people..." My voice trailed off as I sorted through my thoughts. "I know things about people, and sometimes when I talk about someone, it's like I can summon them to me."

She laughed, but it was clear she didn't think it was funny. "Come on, Sloan. Really?"

"Just think about it." I looked at her over the rim of my tumbler and sipped my drink.

She was quiet for a while. There were a thousand odd events she could have been replaying in her mind. Like, the time I said I wanted Jason Ward to ask me to the homecoming dance, and he was waiting by my locker after class. Or, when I told her I had a bad feeling about our gym teacher, and we found out on Monday he had died of a heart attack over the weekend. Finally, she looked at me again. "You know I wouldn't believe a word of this if I hadn't known you for so long."

I nodded. "I don't believe it most of the time myself."

"When you say you 'know' people. What do you know? Like, do you know that guy?" She pointed at the bartender.

I laughed. "No. It's just a sense I get. I can tell you he's an OK guy, but I'm not a mind reader."

She drummed her long nails on the countertop. "So you're psychic?"

"No, I don't think so. I just seem to be able to read people really well."

She leaned toward me and dramatically fanned her fingers like a magician. "And make people suddenly appear!"

"Shhhh!" I looked cautiously around.

Luke, who was waiting nearby, caught my eye and started in our direction.

Adrianne extended her long arm to stop him. "Not so fast, you little eager beaver."

I laughed, and the tension finally started to drain from my shoulders. After a moment, I gripped her arm. "You're not gonna get all freaked out on me now, are you? I haven't told anyone about this since I was old enough to know better."

Her head snapped back with surprise. "Old enough to know better?"

I ran my fingers across the faint scar just above my right eyebrow. "Kids can be pretty cruel when they find out you're different. When I was eight and we still lived in Atlanta, one of them threw a big rock at me during recess."

She gasped. "That's horrible!"

I nodded. "After that, Mom and Dad decided it would be best to move."

"So they know about what you can do?"

she asked.

I shook my head. "Not exactly. Whatever is wrong with me can't be explained by science, so I think it scares them to talk about it. They haven't brought it up once since we moved here." I touched my scar again. "And seven stitches in the face taught me to keep my mouth shut."

She squeezed my hand, her eyes no longer judgmental. "Well, I'm not going to freak out, and I'm not going to tell anyone."

I sighed. "Thank you."

She grinned over the top of her glass. "No one would believe me anyway."

"I know."

Suddenly, she perked up with a wild smile. "What about Brad Pitt?"

I raised my eyebrows. "What about him?"

"Can you get him here?"

I laughed. "That's not the way it works!"

She crossed her arms over her chest. "How do you know?"

I smiled. "Because I've already tried."

**Get The Soul Summoner Series at all major online retailers.**

**The Soul Summoner Series** is available
wherever books are sold online: Amazon, Apple iBooks,
Barnes & Noble, Kobo, and more!

*"Words cannot describe how enjoyable I found this
story. The Soul Summoner is witty, clever and fast
paced... Really, this book has it all: Characters you
fall in love with, an exciting and unpredictable
storyline and humor."* - Juliet Lyons

*"The Soul Summoner is an incredible read. Easy
dialogue. Intriguing mystery. A spicy love triangle. It
will leave you asking, 'When is the next book in the
series coming out?'"* - M. Robinson

*"The Soul Summoner, by Elicia Hyder, caught my
interest in the first two chapters and never let go."* -
RK. Close

## Other Books by Elicia Hyder

### The Bed She Made

2015 Watty Award Winner for Best New Adult Romance

### To Be Her First

The Young Adult Prequel to The Bed She Made